PRAISE FOR
THE LAST ONE

"The musical quality of the novel is key—the story races along with the pace of a song or a poem...Daas's depiction of Paris has been hailed by critics...Her beautifully drawn descriptions of endless hours on public transport were Daas's way of exploring a commute she once considered 'normal,' then grew to see as an 'injustice.' Daas's overriding message is that you don't have to give up any part of yourself: you can inhabit a host of seemingly clashing identities at once." —*The Guardian*

"Fatima Daas's monologue is constructed by fragments, as though she were updating Barthes and Mauriac for Clichy-sous-Bois. She carves out a portrait, like a patient, attentive sculptor...or like a mine searcher, aware that each word could make everything explode, and you have to choose them with infinite care."

—Virginie Despentes, author of *King Kong Theory*

"*The Last One* is a thoughtful examination of a character who deeply wants to be known despite lacking the tools to do any of that self-excavation. The work is tender and sweet, lyrically built, and reprises itself in fascinating ways. Who are we apart from our family? Can we face ourselves? Can we love? Fatima Daas asks these questions the way many of us do: plaintively, longingly, and with a tremendous amount of heart."

—Kristen Arnett, author of *Mostly Dead Things* and *With Teeth*

"In *The Last One*, Fatima Daas uses words like bold and vivid brush strokes, exploring identity through lyricism. I tore through this incredible work of art in one sitting, but I often took a moment to catch my breath and admire the defiant beauty at the heart of this book."

—Abdi Nazemian, author of Stonewall
Honor Book *Like a Love Story*

"Fatima Daas' debut novel signals the presence of an exciting voice that commands attention and insists on complexity. Whether she is unpacking family ties or tracing the ways queerness dovetails with other identities, Daas stops you in your tracks with what seems like a quiet symphony until you realize it is in fact a crescendo of what it means to be human."

—Mona Eltahawy, author of *The Seven Necessary
Sins for Women and Girls*

"Whether dealing with chronic illness, sexuality, therapy, education, faith, friendship, family, romance, or riding the bus, Fatima Daas' *The Last One* takes on the world with honesty, humor, and lyricism. The specificity of life in the Parisian suburb of Clichy-sous-Bois underscores universal themes and utterly recognizable emotions. Daas bares her narrator's soul, and we can't look away." —Eman Quotah, author of *Bride of the Sea*

"Daas explores multifaceted identity through achronological slices of life, arrayed like glittering shards of a fractured mirror. An extraordinary debut novel you'll never forget."

—Forsyth Harmon, author of *Justine*

"*The Last One* is a bombshell that examines the question of identity with subtlety and passion." —*Elle* (France)

"A rhythm that pulses, sentences that crack, chapters like a chant...The furiously contemporary voice that we were hoping for." —*Les Inrockuptibles*

"A first novel of striking lyricism, with a narrator on the ridge between the 'forbidden' and her desire." —*Livres Hebdo*

THE LAST ONE

THE LAST ONE

Fatima Daas

TRANSLATED FROM THE FRENCH
BY LARA VERGNAUD

OTHER PRESS

NEW YORK

Originally published in French as *La petite dernière* in 2020
by Les éditions Noir sur Blanc, Paris and Lausanne
Copyright © Les éditions Noir sur Blanc, 2020
Translation copyright © Lara Vergnaud, 2021

Production editor: Yvonne E. Cárdenas
Text designer: Jennifer Daddio / Bookmark Design & Media Inc.
This book was set in Cochin by Alpha Design & Composition
of Pittsfield, NH

1 3 5 7 9 10 8 6 4 2

Library of Congress Cataloging-in-Publication Data
Names: Daas, Fatima, 1995- author. | Vergnaud, Lara, translator.
Title: The last one / Fatima Daas ; translated from the French by Lara Vergnaud.
Other titles: Petite dernière. English
Description: New York : Other Press, [2021] | Originally published in French
as La petite dernière in 2020 by Les éditions Noir sur Blanc, Paris and Lausanne.
Identifiers: LCCN 2021020210 (print) | LCCN 2021020211 (ebook) |
ISBN 9781635421842 (paperback ; acid-free paper) | ISBN 9781635421859 (ebook)
Subjects: LCGFT: Novels in verse.
Classification: LCC PQ2704.A22 P4813 2021 (print) | LCC PQ2704.A22 (ebook) |
DDC 843/.92—dc23
LC record available at https://lccn.loc.gov/2021020210
LC ebook record available at https://lccn.loc.gov/2021020211

THE LAST ONE

My name is Fatima.

The name of a symbolic figure in Islam.

A name that must be honored.

A name that mustn't be "soiled," as we say in my house.

In my house, to soil means to dishonor. *Wassekh*, in Algerian Arabic.

Or *darja, darija*, our word for dialect.

Wassekh: soil, stir shit up, blacken.

It has multiple meanings, like "close."

My mother would use the same word to tell me I had gotten my clothes dirty, the same word when she came home and found her Kingdom in bad shape.

Her Kingdom: the kitchen.

Where we had best stay out of her way.

My mother hated when things weren't put back in their place.

There were rules in the kitchen, like everywhere else. We were expected to know and respect them.

If we couldn't, we had to stay out of the Kingdom.

Among the phrases my mother said all the time, there was this one: *Makènch li ghawèn, fi haði ðar, izzèðolèk.*

It sounded like a punch line to me.

"Not a soul to help you in this house, yet it keeps piling on."

Curling my toes in my knee-high socks, I usually retorted the same way:

"You need to tell me if you need help. I'm not psychic. I can't just guess."

To which my mother would snap back that she didn't need "our" help. She deliberately used the collective pronoun in her reproach, so I wouldn't take it personally, so I wouldn't feel attacked.

My mother started cooking at fourteen.

First, the things she called *ɔahline*: easy.

Couscous, *tchouktchouka*, *ðjouwèz*, lamb tagine with prunes, chicken tagine with olives.

At fourteen, I didn't know how to make my bed.

At twenty, I didn't know how to iron a shirt.

At twenty-eight, I didn't know how to prepare plain spaghetti.

I didn't like hanging out in the kitchen, unless it was to eat.

I liked to eat, but not just anything.

My mother cooked for the whole family.

She designed the menu based on our whims.

I refused meat; I got fish. My father couldn't go without it; there'd be plenty on his plate.

If Dounia, my older sister, wanted fries rather than a traditional meal, that's what she would get.

For as far back as I can remember, I see my mother in the kitchen, hands chapped by the cold, cheeks hollow, drawing a ketchup stick figure over my pasta, decorating the dessert, preparing the tea, storing the pans in the oven.

I only have a single image left: our feet under the table, heads bent over our food.

My mother at the stove, the last to sit down.

Kamar Daas had a Kingdom, but I didn't belong in it.

My name is Fatima Daas.

The name of a girl from Clichy who crosses the tracks to get to school.

I buy a copy of the *Direct Matin* at the Raincy-Villemomble station before I catch the 8:33 a.m. train. I lick my finger to efficiently turn the pages. The headline on page 31: How to Relax.

I find my horoscope beneath the weather forecast.

On the platform, I read my daily horoscope and then the one for the week.

If you want to be able to endure life, prepare for death. —Sigmund Freud

Your astral landscape: Don't beat yourself up if you can't help everyone who asks. Focus on yourself! Think before jumping into major projects. Don't confuse your optimism for Herculean abilities.

WORK: It's time to make some robust decisions. Your realistic approach will be your best asset today by far.

LOVE: If you're in a relationship, be careful not to push away your partner with excessive demands. If you're single, dream about Prince Charming all you want, but don't expect to bump into him on the street corner.

Then I skim through the tragedies of the world as I try to ignore the urge to stare at people on the train.

Every single day there are commuters who refuse to move down the aisles. In the morning, I repeat the same not-magic words: "Would you mind moving forward, please? Other people need to get to work too."
At the end of the day, my tone changes.
I deliberately strip away the politeness.

The commuters who don't move down the aisles are always the ones preparing to get off at the next two stations: Bondy and Noisy-le-Sec.
Their trick is to park themselves next to the doors so they don't miss their stop.

In the bus, I watch to make sure the woman with a child, the pregnant woman, the elderly woman has a place to sit.
I focus my attention exclusively on the women.
I feel like I have to play the vigilante, to defend others, to speak on their behalf, to make them heard, to reassure them, to save them.

I didn't save anyone. Not Nina, not my mother.
Not even myself.
Nina was right.
It's not healthy to want to save the world.

My name is Fatima Daas, but I was born in France, in the department of Yvelines, aka "the 78," in Saint-Germain-en-Laye.

I came into the world by cesarean at the Clinique Saint-Germain on Rue de la Baronne-Gérard.

Cesarean, from the Latin *caedere*: "hew"; "cut."

Incision in the uterus.

After my birth, my mother has a heart attack, at thirty.

I blame myself for being born.

They take me out of her belly at dawn.

I'm not born asthmatic. I become it.

I officially enter the category of allergic asthmatics at age two.

In adolescence, I hear the word "severe" used to describe my condition for the first time.

At seventeen, I understand that I have an invisible disease.

My longest hospital stay lasts six weeks.

My sister Dounia says that I'm a sponge, except the air's not getting out.

It took me a while to realize that my asthmatic episodes can be triggered by emotions.

I have to follow a course of medical treatment, consistently, for life.

Seretide: twice a day, one puff in the morning, one puff at night.

Inorial: one pill in the morning.

Singulair: one pill at night.

Ventoline: in case of respiratory distress.

My name is Fatima.

Fatima is the youngest daughter of the last prophet Mohammed—*Salla Allah alayhi wa salam*, peace and salvation be upon him—and his first wife, Khadidja.

My name is Fatima.
God alone knows if I carry it well.
Whether I've soiled it.

Fatima means "little weaned she-camel."
To wean, in Arabic: *fatm*.
Stop the nursing of a child or a young animal to transition it to a new mode of feeding; feel frustration; separate someone from something or something from someone or someone from someone.

Like Fatima, I should have had three sisters.
One of mine passed away a few hours after her birth.
Her name was Soumya.

Fatima's father deems her the noblest woman in heaven.

The prophet Mohammed—may God's peace and blessings be upon him—said one day: "Fatima is a part of me. Any who harm her harm me."

My father would never say such a thing.

My father doesn't say much to me anymore.

My name is Fatima.

I'm a little weaned she-camel.

I'm the *mazoziya*, the youngest daughter.

The last one.

Before me, there were three girls.

My father had hoped I would be a boy.

During my childhood, he calls me *wlidi*, my little son.

Though he should call me *benti*, my daughter.

He often says: "You're not my daughter."

I reassure myself by understanding that I'm his son.

My mother dresses me until I'm twelve years old.

She puts me in flower dresses, skater skirts, ballet flats. I have headbands in different colors, shaped like crowns.

Not every little girl wants to be a princess, Mama.

I hate everything that has to do with the female universe as my mother presents it to me, but I haven't realized it yet.

Sometimes, my father takes me to school.
He doesn't check my homework.
He doesn't ask me what I learned.
He counts on my mother to do that.

My mother often says: "I did my *wajeb*."
Wajeb: role.
Her role as a mother.

A role: a function served by someone; an attribution assigned to an institution; a collection of norms and expectations that govern the behavior of an individual as a result of their social status or function within a group.
My father doesn't mention his *wajeb*.

My mother would rather I wear sports bras than regular ones. She finds it less "rushed."
She doesn't want me to shave either.
Dounia tells her to let me shave my armpits at least, until I get older.
My mother repeats that I'll have time for all that.

Before I became a teenager, my father would sing me songs.
He would tell me stories too.
Loundja! Loundja, the princess with golden hair.
My father always began his story with once upon a time.

Once upon a time there was Loundja.

A princess who was kept prisoner since she was a small child by *el ghoula*, the ogress, in the highest tower of her fortress, with no door or window. The ogress used Loundja's long hair to climb up the tower.

One night, to no great surprise, a prince discovers Loundja.

He falls in love. He returns to save her. He marries her.

As in many other stories, Loundja and the prince have lots of children and live happily ever after.

What I liked the most was the time my father took to describe in detail Loundja's long golden hair.

When he wasn't telling me the story of Loundja, he would recount the life of the prophet Youssef—*Alayi Salem*, may salvation be upon him.

He always told the part about the prophet's brothers. Eaten up by jealousy, they decided to throw Youssef down a deep well.

My father would whisper in my ear: *Balak yiderolek kima Youssef.* Careful your sisters don't do the same to you!

I had trouble telling the difference between my father's jokes and his warnings.

Early afternoons brought the nap ordeal.

I'd throw tantrums so nobody would force me to sleep.

Then, I figured out that I needed to be clever to get what I wanted.

I found the trick. No need for teary eyes, or even to expend any energy.

And it worked every time.

My father would bring me into the living room. We would lie down side by side in front of the television, my head on his shoulder. My hand on his head.

My father would fall asleep first.

He took the nap I was meant to.

I'd join Dounia and Hanane playing in the garden.

My mother was still in the kitchen.

My name is Fatima.

I have allergic asthma.

The doctors say that I'm not taking my treatment "seriously."

Sometimes I forget my medicine.

Or decide to stop taking it because of the unwanted side effects.

Or decide to stop taking it for other reasons.

Or the opposite. I decide not to respect the prescribed dosage, to take multiple puffs of Ventoline, which provokes an accelerated heart rate.

I've swallowed the same pills multiple times a day, almost since I was born, and there doesn't appear to be any end in sight.

They say that forgetting my medicine is the same thing as refusing to take care of myself, my body, my health.

"They" are the ones who try to make me understand my illness, which I don't.

Pulmonologists, doctors, nurses, physiotherapists.

I think about Monique Lebrun, who was my
primary doctor for ten years, until she retired.

I think about her and the others I met at the hospital
in their white or blue coats, the ones who taught me to
breathe correctly, like everybody else.

"Are you ready? Okay, let's begin. Breathe in with
your nose as you fill your lungs with air. Now breathe
out with your mouth, there you go, gentle. That's it, just
like that, very good, sweetheart."

I hate being called "sweetheart."

Most of the time during the visits, I don't
understand anything Monique is saying. I feel like
she's stuck in the nineteenth century.

She quotes Baudelaire and Rimbaud.

She speaks the same language as them.

Dr. Lebrun wears shirts buttoned all the way up.

It's hard to make out her neck.

So I imagine it.

I can't help furtively glancing at her drooping chest.

Impossible to distinguish her round breasts from
her flabby belly.

Her glasses are always hanging around her neck.

She has trembling hands when she gives me my
prescription.

On November 24, Monique decides to increase the dose of my medicine.

Obligatory switch from Seretide Diskus 250 to Seretide Diskus 500.

My name is Fatima Daas.

I'm French.

I'm of Algerian descent.

My parents and my two older sisters were born in Algeria.

I'm *rebeu*, Arab, and therefore Muslim.

My mother is Muslim.

My father is Muslim.

My sisters, Dounia and Hanane, are Muslim.

We are a family of Muslim Arabs.

We should have been a family of six Muslim Arabs.

The first time that my mother tells me about the death of our older sister, Soumya, I tell her that Soumya was lucky.

In the Muslim religion, if a child dies, they go to heaven.

So I prayed that I would be a Soumya too.

I knew that I wasn't going to be what they call a good Muslim, a true Muslim.

My mother says you're born Muslim.

But I think that I converted.

I think I'm still converting to Islam.

I try to respect my religion as much as I can, to bring myself closer, to make it a way of life.

I like going to my prayer mat, feeling my forehead against the ground, seeing myself prostrate, submissive to God, imploring Him, sensing how miniscule I am before His grandeur, His love, His omnipresence.

My name is Fatima.

The name of a girl from Clichy who spends more than three hours a day on public transportation.

In the RER, the train that goes from Paris to the banlieues and back again, a scrawny hand clings to the door.

A man is holding a fluorescent-green water bottle.

Attention à la marche en descendant du train.

The passengers standing up try to keep their balance.

You can hold on to the handrail, lean against the doors, glue yourself to a window and watch for passengers about to liberate their seats. Or grab the arm of a friend, if you have one.

Por favor, no olvide recoger todo su equipaje.

Some people count the stations.

Some argue over the phone.

Some wear backpacks.

Some laugh loudly, drawing attention.

Some spy on their neighbors' screens.

Some, seated, buried in their phone, tablet, or book, ignore everything around them.

There are strollers and suitcases.

"An incident has been reported. All trains are being held temporarily."

My name is Fatima Daas, but I was born in Yvelines.

When I'm eight years old, we leave the 78 for the 93.

We leave Saint-Germain-en-Laye to move to a town of Muslims: Clichy-sous-Bois.

Outside of my family, the people I grow up with in Clichy-sous-Bois, my neighbors, my friends, my classmates, are almost all Muslim. So it doesn't bother me to be a "Muslim."

At eight years old, I think that:

All North Africans are Muslim.

Muslims are people who don't eat pork and who observe Ramadan.

Fasting means putting yourself in the place of those who have nothing to eat.

Muslims don't drink.

North Africans marry each other, have children, then grandchildren.

I'm in elementary school when I observe Ramadan for the first time.

It's winter.

I don't fast the whole month, I fast in my own way: half days.

I hate eating in the morning.

I feel nauseated and I skip breakfast, even when my mother insists.

Sometimes she stays in the kitchen to make sure I drink the bowl of milk she sets out for me.

As soon as her back is turned, I throw it in the sink.

The first time I observe Ramadan, I understand right away what it feels like to belong.

Like everyone in my family, I'm fasting.

At eleven-thirty, school lets out for lunch.

I go home.

My mother asks me if I'm holding up okay.

My stomach answers for me: "Is there any *chorba* and *brik* left from yesterday?"

My name is Fatima Daas.

My father's name is Ahmed. *Ahmad*: worthy of praise.

My mother, Kamar, the moon.

He, Ahmed, has black eyes, like me.

We have the same eyes.

Black eyes exist.

Ahmed is over six feet tall. Every day, when he goes out the door, he has to remember to duck his head, but occasionally he forgets and then he bumps against the wall.

I laugh quietly behind him. My mother too.

Kamar Daas smells of chamomile. She has a very keen nose.

When I started to smoke, she detected it right away.

Outside, Ahmed walks with his head high and his chest puffed.

Kamar, eyes on the ground.

She has a Greek profile and tiny slits for nostrils.

Sometimes, I want to call Ahmed Daas *Abi*, "my father," and sometimes I can't bring myself to.

My mother is shorter than me, under five foot four. She has large rosy cheeks and the hands of a mason.

My father has eight brothers and sisters. My mother, ten.

My mother left her family to follow my father to France.

My mother isn't just a housewife, isn't just a stay-at-home mom, isn't just a mom.

My name is Fatima Daas.

I was born by cesarean at the Clinique Saint-Germain on Rue de la Baronne-Gérard.

Cesarean, *caedere*: "hew"; "cut."

Incision in the uterus.

At twenty-five, I meet Nina.

Nina, Celtic for "summit," Hebrew for "grace."

Saint Nina spread the Christian religion throughout Georgia in the fourth century.

But Nina Gonzalez is not a saint or a Christian.

I think that Nina is a symbolic figure in my story.

The first time I see Nina, she immediately intrigues me.

She puts her hands in the back pockets of her jeans.

Her sunglasses, on top of her head, hold back her hair.

When she's not wearing her sunglasses, she lets a few strands cover part of her face. Then, only one eye remains visible.

The right one.

Above it is one dark eyebrow, the same shade as her hair.

Nina hides under somber clothes.
Black clothes.

People guess different backgrounds for her, but not the right ones.

She answers yes when a coworker asks if she has "Indian blood," yes when someone else thinks she's Haitian.

She has a slender, dynamic body.
Her steps light and agile.
Nina doesn't sit.
Not for long.
Most of the time, she's in motion.

She smokes rolled cigarettes, she drinks coffee.
She smokes joints and drinks beer.
When she's not smoking rolled cigarettes, she smokes Marlboro Reds.

There's a fragile look in her eyes: unsure, uncertain, hard and delicate, gentle.

Her eyes are brown, almost black, brooding.

She switches back and forth from levity to seriousness.

She laughs at everything, at others and especially herself.

She says that laughter protects.

She doesn't answer questions.

She says she doesn't know why she doesn't answer questions.

I think it's because she doesn't trust me, others, and especially not herself.

Nina's the only one who asks if I'm okay, several times in the same sentence, repeatedly in the same day.

She'll leave me memories scattered throughout Clichy-sous-Bois, Paris, and elsewhere.

Nina is seated to my left.

I'm seated to her right.

We're under a tree, its bowed branches surrounding us.

The sky is clear and the sun fierce.

The heat too.

A pigeon goes by.

It attracts my attention, hers too, and we both turn around, at the same time, as if to watch it fly away.

I stop watching the pigeon.

I see her, still watching it.

A gust of wind goes through us.

She smiles and says, "That feels good."

I watch her.

I dumbly repeat, "That feels good."

I remember sitting in the same spot, with someone else.

A boy whom I didn't watch.

My name is Fatima.
Fatima, little weaned she-camel.

Before my nineteenth birthday, I decide to sign up
for asthma school.
Asthma school is a concept, created in 1991 by the
Asthma & Allergies Association, that aims to provide
a therapeutic education less boring than theoretical
classes.

Before attending, I read a few brochures to know
what to expect.
I learn that this course will enable me to better
understand my condition and to control it.
The school teaches you how to become actively
involved in your care, better understand your triggers,
predict and avoid an asthma attack or keep it from
worsening, and, most importantly, you learn how to
accept your condition.

My name is Fatima.

The name of a symbolic figure in Islam.

A name that mustn't be soiled, a name I have to honor.

My name is Fatima and I sense God everywhere I go, everywhere I am.

I feel His grace envelop me.

When I leave my house in the morning, I recite a prayer:

> I begin with the name of Allah. I trust in Allah.
> There is no protection and no strength but in
> Allah. O Allah, I ask You to keep me from leading
> others astray or being led astray by others. I ask
> You to keep me from sinning or being led into sin
> by others. I ask You to keep me from committing
> injustice or enduring injustice myself.

My name is Fatima Daas.

I'm a liar.

I'm a sinner.

In elementary school, I tell Alexandra and Amina that I'm in love with a boy.

They're my best friends at the time.

The boy's name is Jack.

He's French.

He's blond with green eyes.

At home, I write on a fogged-up window: "Fatima + Jack = Love."

Jack isn't in love with me.

I'm not in love with Jack.

But I'd like to be in love, like Alexandra and Amina.

Alexandra is Portuguese Catholic. Her boyfriend is named Daniel.

Amina is Algerian Muslim, but it's not stamped on her forehead.

Everyone says that her family is "Frenchified," because Amina goes to the music conservatory in Livry, plays piano, and does gymnastics.

Her mother doesn't wear a veil.

Her father doesn't have a long beard.

My name is Fatima.

I'm the girl from the banlieue who observes how the Parisians act.

In the RER, the women lugging around strollers always get the same nasty looks. The women who rarely get any help going down the stairs when there's no elevator, the women nobody lets in front of them on the bus, because it might take forever, the same women people give up their seats to with a twinge of pity.

I say women because most of the time it's a she and not a he pushing the stroller around that early.

People get mad at the mom when the child starts whining.

They turn around, restless; they whisper.

They try to see where the damn crying is coming from.

When they finally find it, they shoot a dirty stare.

A look that says, "Can't you shut your kid up, you dumb bitch?!" Then they turn around with a sigh.

They think very loudly to themselves that she's a bad mother.

My name is Fatima.
I'm asthmatic.
I have an invisible disease.

One time an allergist scolds me for missing a consultation in 1997.
I draw a blank.
I do the math in my head.
I respond that I was five years old at the time.

Ever since I was little, people have been telling me that asthma is a condition that will go away with time.
I can't stand sentences that end in "with time."
I can't stand waiting anymore.

The first session of asthma school is on a Tuesday morning at 10 a.m., in Montfermeil. The town right next to Clichy-sous-Bois.
People mix them up a lot and think the two towns are actually just one. It's not a big deal. We all know each other.

For the most part we went to the same high school. There's just the one, Alfred Nobel High School, between Clichy and Montfermeil, and on the border with Gagny.

When I leave my parents' house, I go up Allée de Bellevue, I walk through a housing complex called Le Hameau de la Verrière, a shortcut to the bus stop. No one says "de la Verrière." People just say the "Hameau."

I take the 613 or 601, I can't remember which, the first one to arrive. It stops in front of the hospital. All I have to do is cross the sidewalk and enter the mustard-yellow lobby that makes me nauseous every time.

Room B2. There's a group of four people already sitting at a rectangular conference table, of different genders and ages, the doctor and the nurse, standing beside the door, coffee and tea on the table, with Bonne Maman madeleines bought at Carrefour.

They were waiting on me. The session begins like any session, with introductions. We go around the table, like any time you have to talk without wanting to. I dubbed it the Alcoholics Anonymous intro. You have to identify yourself. Provide the strict minimum: in this case, nothing more than your first name, last name, and age, three things you don't choose.

We have the same problem, the same condition.

That's one of the reasons they bring us together, so that we feel less alone. They tell us that it's crucial to listen to other people's experiences and to share our own.

I don't share anything.

Later that morning, a clinical psychologist comes by.

When she arrives, the doctor and the nurse leave the room.

"Let's stick to first names. You can call me Clarisse. Please feel free to speak up, to interrupt me whenever you feel like it."

Right away, she lets us know we're going to be buddy-buddy.

She has big blue eyes, sky blue or sea blue. Both. Same thing.

Clarisse talks about the "paternalistic" syndrome afflicting certain doctors. That sounds right to me, well said, it comes out nicely from her V-shaped mouth.

I nod yes to everything she says, without uttering a word.

When Clarisse, with her big smile, asks me if I want to say something, I gently refuse.

After an hour with the psychologist, Mrs. Cerisier, the nurse, knocks on the door. Whenever Mrs. Cerisier talks, she rubs her index finger behind her ear. It's one of her obsessive-compulsive tics that she can't suppress.

During the practical workshops, we're taught to measure our DEP, our *débit expiratoire de pointe*, which means peak expiratory flow. But rather than saying "D-E-P," the nurse says *dep*, the same as French slang for fag.

Every time she says *dep*, I make a dumb little smile.

There're no other idiotically happy fools in the group. Except me.

I look down, I start casually scribbling something on my sheet of paper, but I realize that the four others are focused on Mrs. Cerisier, who's explaining how to use the DEP device.

It allows you to control your breathing.

My name is Fatima Daas.

I'm Muslim, therefore I'm afraid:

That God doesn't love me.

That He doesn't love me the way I love Him.

That He'll abandon me.

Of not being the person I'm "supposed" to be.

Of questioning what God has commanded me to do.

Of being left to my own devices.

Of waking up in the middle of the night, terrified.

I speak to Allah, the All-Forgiving, when I do my five prayers.

Sometimes I lose my concentration.

Sometimes I drown in my thoughts.

I try to re-center myself, to detach myself from this earthly existence that appears to be my main preoccupation.

I cherish this exchange with Allah.

God doesn't need me to pray for Him.

It's me who needs it.

I think I may be a hypocrite.
I sinned.
I stopped sinning.
I sinned again.
My name is Fatima Daas.
I'm a sinner.

My name is Fatima.

I'm Muslim.

Sometimes, during my commute, I try to recite the *∂hikr*, but all the mixed-together voices trickle in. I melt instead into the noise of the train cars, into Parisian conversations, into the smells of sweat, alcohol, and perfume.

Excuse me, I'd like to get off. Shit! I can't find my ticket. That child is the god-awful worst. He won't let up. I'm getting off at the next stop. Hey girl, looking good. Can you open the window, please? I'm getting crushed here. Just forget it, I'm hanging up, you're starting to piss me off. We're almost at the Gare du Nord, relax, everyone's gonna get off. Why is he staring at me like that? Pervert! Mom, how many stations left? I feel like I'm suffocating. Morning, folks, I'm sorry to bother you during your ride, but the thing is I've been living on the streets for ten years now. I'll take anything you can give me, meal tickets, change. Thank you, have a nice day.

A woman rolls her scarf up to her nostrils.
The sound of yellow coins in a cup.
Red lipstick, halfway rubbed off.
A man in profile, with a Yamaha hat, grumbles.
Someone stole his seat.
I give him mine.
He says thank you without a glance.

The *∂hikr* is the repetition of God's name in order to remember Him.

My name is Fatima.

I have a chronic disease.

A condition that doesn't appear to be going away with time.

As an adult, I wait until the last minute to go to the hospital when I feel my lungs tightening.

As a child, in Clichy-sous-Bois, my asthma attacks are usually triggered at night, during my sleep.

I climb down from the bunk bed quietly, so I don't wake up my sisters, but I'm too clumsy.

I might make the bed squeak as I go down the ladder, step on Dounia, who sleeps on a mattress on the floor, or cough a little too loudly.

Sometimes, all three at the same time.

Once I get out the door, I'm almost saved, all I have to do is turn left to enter my parents' bedroom.

It's closed but never locked.

Neither is ours for that matter.

The TV is still on, Al Jazeera or BFM. I get into my parents' bed, I slide between them.

I separate their already wide-apart bodies.

I'm wheezing. My mother wakes up.

After *salat Sobh*, the first prayer of the day, my father takes me to the hospital in his metallic-gray Mercedes-Benz. I'm half-asleep and still wheezing each time I exhale. My father asks me if it hurts anywhere.

At the hospital, I'm given an aerosol inhaler, four puffs to clear my airways. After every inhalation, my father, sitting on a chair beside the bed, bringing his head near my shoulder, says: *Thèssè darelk haja?* "Can you feel it working?"

My father has little faith in either medicine or education.

My name is Fatima.

Fatima is a girl's name, a Muslim name.

I start to dress "like a boy" at the age of twelve.

I don't know this right away. Someone points it out
to me.

I wear hoodies, sweatpants, Nike Air Maxes.

I pull my hair back into a bun or a ponytail.

I use gel to flatten the tiny hairs that stick out in
front.

My hair is *khrach*, curly, "Arab" hair.

Sometimes I wear a baseball cap that my friend
Moussa lent me one day.

I'll wear it the whole time I'm in middle school, until
Mrs. Salvatore, the disciplinary counselor, confiscates
it for good.

In middle school, we're not allowed headphones or
cell phones.

We're not allowed to wear baseball hats in the hall.

We're not allowed to wear baseball hats at all.

In middle school, I have girlfriends, but I prefer hanging out with boys.

We're a gang of six.

Moussa, Zaidou, and his little brother Moun.

All three are Muslims from the Comoros.

Samir is Moroccan Muslim.

Wilkens is the Christian of the gang.

I'm the only girl in the group, but I don't know it yet.

I'm in gym class the first time I get my period.

I realize that I'm a girl.

I cry.

That night, I tell my mother I don't want it.

She explains that it's natural.

I hate nature.

My name is Fatima Daas, I was born in France,
sometimes I spend more than four hours on public
transportation to get to class, work, a theater, a
museum, or back home to my parents' house.

I begin to take public transportation regularly when
I'm eighteen.

After a while, I experience "commuter fatigue,"
the kind that induces a migraine at pretty much the
same time every evening, that makes you prematurely
realize that your body is aging, that colors your mood,
prompts you to overreact, to complain almost as
much as the Parisians, and to bursts of anger that are
difficult to control.

It's the kind of fatigue that makes you think about
"moving closer."

Moving closer means leaving.
Left: betrayed, renounced, and abandoned.

My name is Fatima.
Fatima Daas.
The name of a symbolic figure in Islam.
Nina Gonzalez is the heroine of my story.

One day, I finally decide to ask Nina out.
I don't suggest we go grab a drink.
That's what everyone does.
I invite her to come see me on stage.
Later, I'll suggest we go grab a drink, go to the theater, go to an exhibition.

"I can get you two tickets if you want to bring someone, Nina."
Nina takes a long drag on her cigarette as she watches me, while I stare at the smoke spreading above her head.
"I wouldn't have any idea how to find a suitable theater friend. Sorry I can't satisfy your curiosity."

Nina comes on her own to watch me, which eases my mind a little.

The lights go out, go on.

I recognize a few faces, including Rokya's, in the second row. Rokya is my best friend.

I spot Nina in the back of the theater, but I don't look at her for long.

Applause rings out. I think I did a good job.

I think I did a good job in front of Nina.

After the show, I find Nina sitting in the lobby. I join her, she gives me a big hug, and she says, "You shine on stage, Fatima."

I spontaneously respond, "Especially when you're in the audience."

I regret saying that a little, because I don't know if she wants to hear it.

She doesn't say anything.

I introduce Nina to my friends.

We spend the rest of the evening together.

My name is Fatima Daas.
I'm a troubled adolescent, a misfit.

Every day in middle school, after lunch, we settle
onto our "turf" at the back of the playground, between
the two white trash cans.
Everyone knows it's our spot.
When we arrive, the other kids automatically leave.
We don't have to ask.

Moun leans against the wall.
Wilkens and Moussa, seated across from each other
on the trash cans, don't make eye contact.
I'm in the middle.
I go from one trash can to the other.

"Keep zigging around like that and people gonna
think you're coked-up, Fati-gangsta."

The ritual begins. We warm up by taking cheap
shots at each other.

Moun starts rapping.
We encourage him by insulting him.

It's winter.
My hands are red.
The wind is crazy strong.

"There's no point sitting out in the cold, guys.
C'mon, let's move, those sons-of-bitches are nice and
warm inside while we're freezing our asses off."

"Those sons-of-bitches" are the enemy camp:
teachers, disciplinary counselors, monitors, anyone
representing authority.

The gang agrees.
I've managed to convince them.
We decide to take a few laps through the halls.
We know we're going to get chased by the
monitors.
We've all already been temporarily suspended from
school.
Except Wilkens, the smartest.

As we walk through the halls, Will tells us he
grinded with some girl the night before.
"Guys, I could feel her pubes."
He acts out the scene, laughing.
I don't add anything to the discussion.

In the days that follow, I feel like I have to talk about somebody.

I say that I'm in love with a boy in our school.

I pick a Tunisian who seems handsome and nice.

His name is Ibrahim.

We were in the same class in sixth grade.

We got into a fight during French.

I can't remember how it started but I know I told him that I was going to make him bleed after class.

He had called me a bitch.

We each got a warning.

That was with Mrs. Benameur.

She got scared that day.

She took my words literally.

Mrs. Benameur had imagined school letting out.

Ibrahim, on the ground, covered in blood.

Me, proud, smiling.

Everyone called her "Mrs. Bend-over."

She had big red glasses that took up half her face.

We nicknamed her Betty, in reference to the show *Ugly Betty*, which came out in France that year.

Another time, she cried because another student and I wouldn't change seats.

It became a whole thing.

Mrs. Benameur left the classroom.

She was pregnant.

I felt bad.

I don't know if it's because she was pregnant.

I didn't admit it, that I felt bad, to anyone.

I bitched to everyone that she was breaking our balls by running to the principal, crying.

Maybe I was fond of Mrs. Benameur.

My name is Fatima.

I'm a girl.

I like boys.

Of course.

One day, I confess that I have a crush on Ibrahim to my friends.

Moun is the first to react. "Shut up! You're a dude, you can't dig another dude. That's sketch, Fatima."

My name is Fatima.

I was born in France.

Saint-Germain-en-Laye: my first steps, my first smile, my first tears.

I haven't turned six yet, in Saint-Germain-en-Laye, and when my father comes home it smells like tobacco mixed with something else.

Something I don't recognize.

Tobacco is my father's cologne.

He smokes inside the apartment. He's not worried about my asthma. He puts me on his knees and holds his cigarette in his left hand.

In the middle of the night, when he comes home late, my father turns on all the lights and clinks dishes in the kitchen.

He finds his dinner prepared and placed in the microwave by my mother.

When he comes back into the living room, which

serves as our five-person bedroom, I take a peek, but I don't take it upon myself to complain.

Once my older sister dares to ask him to turn out the light with a yawn.

He calls her *khamja*—whore, trash—but Dounia keeps talking back. So he walks over and smacks her.

My mother whispers to her, *Soktè.* Shut up!

That happens a lot, my mother telling us to shut up.

She says it because she doesn't want things to spiral.

Plus, things degenerate fast.

When he hits one of us, it rarely ends there.

He'll hit two out of four. Sometimes I'm the only one he doesn't hit.

I see him do it, I get between them, I know he'll win, that at any moment I might find myself in the same position as my sisters. And when he pulls his belt off his jeans, then I know it's time to go, because it leaves red marks on my legs, which I think are really ugly, but mainly because they sting for days and there's no way to make it go away.

I slip away, sobbing. I come back every time I hear one of my sisters cry too loud or let out a scream.

Then I withdraw to a corner, for the second time; thankfully it goes quickly, a few minutes, I hear one or two outbursts, then sobs. And it's over.

The next day everyone acts like nothing happened.

My name is Fatima.
The name of a symbolic figure in Islam.
A name that must be honored.
A name that I dishonored.

When I'm a teenager, I look my father in the eyes.
I tell him, "You're a monster!"
It's the first time I've thought something so strongly.
He hasn't said a word to me since that day and
neither have I.

My name is Fatima Daas.

I write stories so I don't have to live my own.

I'm twelve years old when I go on a school trip to Budapest.

Everyone gathers in the evening to go over the itinerary.

Right after dinner, in a big room where there's no Wi-Fi.

Impossible to connect to MSN or Skyblog, or send a message to kill the boredom.

After the meeting, the teachers give us one free hour before bedtime.

I stay in the big room with Rokya.

She puts her legs on the table.

I do the same.

I have a Happy Families deck in my pocket, so I take it out.

But we didn't play Happy Families at all.

Two classmates joined us: Lola and Murat.

Rokya suggests we play Truth or Dare.

Murat and Lola agree.

I say, "You're on, but we have to do crazy stuff! Not just say 'good night' to a teacher."

Everyone laughs.

"Okay, then you go first, since you're so into it!"

Murat thinks he's intimidating me by saying that, so I act like he can't get to me, like I'm not worried about what he might ask me to do.

I say, sure of myself and overarticulating, "I choose DARE!"

Murat strokes his chin with his right hand, staring up at the ceiling. I have to laugh.

"Okay, get up and give Lola a kiss."

I'm about to stand when Murat finishes his sentence, "ON THE MOUTH," with a grin, as though, by adding that phrase, he's made the dare impossible.

Rokya bursts out laughing. She translates:

"Basically, in case you didn't get it, Fatima, you have to make out with Lola."

"Ugh, you guys are sick! No way. Murat, you're disgusting!"

When I say that, Lola thanks me.

I don't know if I find her pretty. I never thought about it.

"Nah, nah, Lola. This idiot is being mad sketch. It's not you who's disgusting. I wasn't saying that about you."

Lola smiles as she thinks about what she's about to say.

"Okay, okay, relax! I'm happy to take the dare, just to help you out."

I lower my eyes when I hear the word "happy."

I look at her without saying anything, then I lower my eyes again.

"Well, go!" yells Murat. "Go ahead, it's your dare, Lola!"

I've stopped moving.

I'm frozen.

I hear Lola stand up.

She comes over to me.

I think about shoving her.

Knocking her to the ground.

I don't do anything. Luckily.

She would have hit her head against the corner of the table.

Lola gives me a quick, gentle kiss on the lips.

I don't have time to say or do anything and it's already done.

She makes a point of looking at me before she returns to sit in her chair. She says, "Who's next?" with a wink at me.

I'm twelve years old.

I don't understand what just happened.

Rokya is sleeping in the same room as me.

She wanted to give me a hug before we went to bed. I refused.

And then, during the night, alone, there's something that terrifies me.

A thought I don't put into words: I'm going to hell.

I want to get up, join Rokya in her bed, wake her up maybe.

Tell her that I'd like a hug after all.

I don't know how to talk.

So I stay in my bed alone.

I try to think about something else, but then, Lola pops back up.

Lola is a tomboy too, but not like me.

Physically, she looks like a girl.

She found the balance.

I don't think that Lola likes girls.

In any case, we never talked about that game.

And I didn't ever play Truth or Dare again.

My name is Fatima Daas.
The name of a model figure in Islam.

As a child, at home, I recite a surah, *Al-fil*: The Elephant.
This surah has five verses.
I'm going to recite it to my mother, with a strong intonation.
I practiced for at least two hours.
My mother tells me it sounds like the scholar Sheikh Sudais's recitation.
I smile. That's the effect I wanted.

I'd have liked to be an imam, to recite the Koran with the *tajwid*, a chanted reading; to guide the group prayer; listen, advise, hold congresses.
I tell my mother that I want to record myself reading from the Koran, to share it maybe.
She says that it's not allowed.
I don't try to find out why.
I give up.
The Koran soothes me.

My name is Fatima.

I'm a tourist.

The first year, I enjoy my long commute from Clichy-sous-Bois to Paris. From Paris to Clichy-sous-Bois.

I explore this new dimension of space and time. I take advantage of every minute, as if I were gaining time that I don't have the opportunity to use.

My trips are filled with reading, with music.

Sometimes I manage to scribble a few pages in my journal.

When I'm sitting on the metro, I write about others, the people getting on, getting off, slipping through the doors before they close, the sad faces that I want to take with me.

To get to Paris, I need to take different forms of transportation, starting with a bus, any bus, to reach a train station.

Usually, I take the 613 or the 601, which drops me at either the Aulnay-sous-Bois station or Raincy-Villemomble.

They come by every ten minutes.

On the bus, I sit in the first row when it's free, just behind the driver, and actually sometimes it's the same driver, from one day to the next, sometimes twice in the same day.

In the first fifteen seconds, I try to remember where I've seen his or her familiar face. The first thing that comes to me is "bus driver," the person reduced to a job. Like how we call the school employees "library lady" or "cafeteria lady."

It's a delicious feeling to recognize a face, a voice, an expression, a gesture.

My name is Fatima.
It's meant to be a peaceful name.
I think I've soiled it.

One evening at school, during senior year, I bully a
boy.
His name is Benjamin.
When he talks, his hands move too.
He's pale, thin, effeminate.

Benjamin walks by me and I trip him.
He stumbles, straightens up, looks at me, and asks
me why I did that.
I tell him to get lost before I lose my temper.
He raises his voice and repeats his question in an
indignant tone.

"Are you seriously talking to me, you little fag?
Move before I fuck you up!"

The four people who are next to me laugh a little but also try to calm me down.

Benjamin leaves, crying.
I could almost kill myself.

Two years later, I run into Benjamin in Clichy-sous-Bois.
I think about what I did.
I think about what I've become.
I can't summon the strength to apologize.

My name is Fatima Daas.
I'm French.
I'm Algerian.
I'm French of Algerian descent.

The first time I visit Algeria, I'm in fifth grade.

For weeks before the trip, I develop a mental picture of the people, the smells, the colors.

The time has come to meet "the family."

All the faceless individuals who are part of my parents' past.

A past they don't talk about.

For weeks before the trip, we prepare suitcases of gifts.

I say "we" to feel involved.

My parents buy clothes, shoes, purses, perfume, for every member of the family.

For the youngest: toys and candy.

For the boys: Playmobil sets, weapons, balls, cars, and trucks.

For the girls: baby dolls and Barbies.

My parents ask their respective families if they need something in particular. They say they don't need anything.

What matters most is our presence.

My parents understand that they have to insist.

I didn't understand yet.

Eventually, during phone chats, my Algerian relatives spit it out.

They have many needs, which they express in a coded way.

We call this *mghané*: to make something implicitly understood.

When my paternal aunts see their presents, they say this one is better than that one, that it cost more, that it's prettier, that they would have preferred a purse rather than a veil or nothing at all rather than perfume.

My maternal aunts choose their presents themselves.

The same ritual is performed at the end of every trip.

My parents give money in an envelope to their brothers and sisters.

My parents fight a little to get my aunts and uncles to accept.

Now I know the end of the story.

Their families finally accept the money and spend it very quickly.

As an adult, back in France, I write in a notebook: "It's like I'm leaving a part of myself in Algeria, but every time I tell myself that I won't be going back."

My name is Fatima Daas.
I feel like I'm living a double life.

I leave the hospital in Montfermeil after a ten-day hospitalization.
Rokya's waiting for me in the cafeteria.
I take the elevator hoping it's the last time.
During my stay, I write in a notebook:
"Hospitals are kind of like prisons. You count the number of visitors. You resent the ones who didn't come. You resent him—Ahmed Daas."

I reach the cafeteria. Rokya is sitting, legs slightly spread, holding a can of Oasis Tropical and a plastic cup.

"Roky, before you even ask me if I'm okay, I'm not."
She takes me in her arms and hugs me really hard.
I still wheeze every time I exhale.
She hands me a vending-machine coffee, telling me she still doesn't get how I can drink this crap.

I tell her that it wakes me up or that it relaxes me, I don't remember.

"I need to tell you something, Roky. I mean damn, ten days locked up, I've had time to think."

Rokya looks at me. I can read curiosity mixed with concern in her eyes.

She says nothing. She listens.

We get up, we trade the smell of the hospital for the smell of wet earth, we walk all the way to the arboretum.

There are big clouds, and we figure it'll start raining soon but we don't care.

I admit to Rokya, a little embarrassed, that I signed up for some dating sites.

"It's a good way to put yourself out there but also stay hidden."

"Umm, Fatima, you're a weird romantic. Those sites aren't gonna do anything for you. They won't work. Plus, you might end up with some real dickheads."

I cut Rokya off before she gets too far.

"I don't want to meet guys, Roky."

I say this like how I'd say I need to buy some bread. And then, Rokya looks at me, I see a proud little smile form in the corners of her mouth, and she says, "So what, you want to meet a hamster or something?"

When she says that, her little smile takes up all the room, and then that's all you can see.

Rokya starts laughing, and her whole body shakes.

The image of a hamster jumps into my mind, so I start laughing too. But I quickly compose myself.

"Roky, don't make me say it, please!"

She says I don't need to talk.

So we stop talking. We walk around the park one last time, in silence. We get to the exit. Rokya blocks my path. I look at her and dumbly say, "Well, what? There a hamster on my head?"

We burst out laughing at the same time. And it's in those moments that I love her even more.

"Fatima, there are no hamsters in Clichy, or actually, there are, obviously, they exist, but they're hiding, like you."

With a big smile, I say, "Bye, Roky, I'm going hamster-hunting."

My name is Fatima Daas.

Before I allowed myself to write, I satisfied others' expectations.

After high school, I enroll in an intensive college prep program in literature.

It's what good students do in France.

They go to med school or do a multiyear prep program or go straight to Sciences Po.

For several months, I imitate my classmates.

I have to:

Work for several hours after classes end for the day.

Learn dates and definitions by heart.

Take exam after exam.

Read and analyze texts written exclusively by white hetero cis men.

I walk into my first class of the day. It's a Wednesday. It's 8:30 a.m.

The Spanish professor hands us back our

homework. He holds on to mine. He looks at me with
his big glasses.

"Miss Daas, would you step outside with me for a
minute?"

I stand up and push my chair under my table.
I sense his impatience.
I don't have time to grab my jacket.
I follow him, dumbly.
He's already outside, the door closed.
Two, three students watch me go.
I'm in a T-shirt, so I feel the wind stroking my arms,
my hairs stand on end, it tickles.

"So... Miss Daas [he says this in a strong, manly
voice, looking me straight in the eyes], I'm not going to
do anything, you don't have to worry, but I just want
to know the truth [he takes a shitty dramatic pause].
Who did your work?"
I don't entirely understand so I say, smiling, "My
homework?"
He answers, "Yes, your homework. Who did it for
you?"
Sometimes, when people doubt me, I start doubting
myself. It's weird, I make up scenarios that make
it so they're right, but, this time, I didn't feel like it
because the work had been easy and I hadn't taken any
pleasure in doing it.

I didn't answer.

I was hoping he would say it was an April Fools'
joke in February, anything really, but he wasn't the
kind of guy to joke around. I still thought he'd take it
back, that he would sense, from my silence, that he was
the big fucking joke.

He started up again, "Okay, very well, who helped
you?"

I was getting tired, but I still answered, "I love
Spanish. My average last year was 18/20, and I got 16
on the *baccalauréat*."

Then I realized that justifying, proving, legitimizing
myself, showing my worth wasn't a fate shared by the
other students who were inside, in the warmth. No one
had to argue for ten minutes, in a T-shirt, in the cold,
to prove that they had in fact deserved a 17/20.

One month later, I dropped out of the program.
I didn't go to med school.
I didn't get into Sciences Po.
I wrote.

My name is Fatima Daas.

The name of a girl from Clichy who has to make at least three transfers to get to her university.

When traffic is light, I reach the train station in fifteen minutes.

I have to switch to the RER, the B when I end up at Aulnay station.

The E when I'm at Raincy.

The first year, I arrive early for my meetings, whether they're personal, medical, or professional.

The second year, I arrive on time.

The third year, I arrive late.

The fourth year, I don't arrive.

I don't read anymore. I listen to music that goes along with my thoughts.

I force myself not to fall asleep, for fear I'll reach the end of the line.

I'm afraid I'll have to start over again.

I get nauseated when I sit backward on the RER.

I know now that long commutes favor rambling thoughts.

I get the direction wrong a lot.

I remember strangers.

I've already seen the same person multiple times, on the same metro.

I've already dreamt of that person.

I try not to believe in signs anymore.

I try not to see signs everywhere anymore.

I think I might be superstitious.

I think that's not allowed.

My name is Fatima.

The first time I consult a psychologist, I'm seventeen years old.

It's not my parents' idea.

No one in my family knows that I'm seeing a shrink.

It doesn't sink in for me either.

My psychologist, Mrs. Guérin, usually wears a white coat that goes down to her knees. Underneath her coat, a black skirt with dark tights, a yellow or black turtleneck, a white button-up shirt. She wears her hair down. It's short, wavy, blond.

At the first session with Mrs. Guérin, I say three sentences in all.

The second session, I spend my time destroying a pencil sharpener.

The third session, I decide to stop.

I eventually go back.

I see Mrs. Guérin eight times in two months.

One sixty-minute session per week.

The first three meetings, I get to the door and act like one of those characters in a movie, going back to see their ex.

I bring my fist right up to the door. I get ready to knock.

I take a deep breath.

And I let it out.

Then, rewind.

My arm falls along my body.

I stay there, staring at the door, for sixty seconds.

I take a step back, as if to say "I'm out of here."

Mrs. Guérin, on the other side, knows perfectly well I'm out here flailing about, waiting for her to decide for me.

Sometimes she doesn't make things easy for me. She calls me back once I've done a one-eighty.

"You know, I can hear you when you come up the stairs. You might not wear heels but you make an awful racket and in fact you let me know you're here without even trying."

Mrs. Guérin knew what the problem was.

I left so someone would hold me back.

My name is Fatima.
My parents are Muslim.
My sisters are Muslim.
We are a family of five Muslim Arabs.

In my teens, I remember my parents being
pragmatic.
Islam meant believing in God, loving Him, fearing
Him, obeying Him.
I got the first stages right.

I loved God, His messenger, my mother times three,
then my father.
That was the order I had to give my rankings in
whenever my father caught me off guard.

"Who do you love first? Second? And then?"

If I got the order wrong—it only happened once—
I'd have to stay in a corner of the living room with a

dictionary on my head until Ahmed Daas decided to give me back my freedom.

Ahmed, "worthy of praises."

It's said that a man came to see Allah's messenger—may the peace and blessings of Allah be upon him.

"O messenger of God! Who is most deserving of my good company?"
"Your mother."
The man continued, "Then who?"
"Your mother."
The man asked again, "Then who?"
"Your mother."
"Then who?" asked the man one last time.
"Then your father."

One morning, before middle school, in front of the mirror, I cover my hair with gel. I spread it delicately. My mother surprises me. She comes in and it's as if she caught me rifling through her purse or setting the house on fire.
My mother says, "God created man and woman. God doesn't like it when a girl wants to look like a boy."
For once, she talks to me in French.
I don't respond that morning.
I don't kiss her goodbye.
I leave the house with knots in my stomach.

My name is Fatima Daas.

I was in therapy for four years.

It's my longest relationship.

At twenty-five, I meet Nina Gonzalez.

At the time, I think I'm polyamorous.

I'm seeing two women, Gabrielle and Cassandra.

I find what's missing in one in the other, without knowing what it is.

I feel like my life is just beginning to have a semblance of stability.

Cassandra is twenty-two years old.

Gabrielle is thirty-five.

Cassandra is "too little" for me.

My best friend Rokya teases me, "So turns out you're into cougars, Fatima!"

I ran into Cassandra several times in LGBTQI+ circles before I dared approach her.

She struck me immediately as a breath of fresh air, uninhibited, innocent.

Cassandra didn't come across as a lesbian, not when it came to a dress code, or group values, or overinflated feminist ambitions.

We immersed ourselves in the lesbian world, women-only happy hours, Barbi(e)turix parties, queer nights at La Java.

I thought of these places as refuges.

Cassandra and I both took time off work for Gay Pride.

An activist friend, who heard me boasting about it, grabbed me by the arm to correct me.

"PRIDE, Fatima! Not Gay Pride. You make lesbians and everyone else in the community invisible when you say Gay Pride."

There was gentleness in her voice, and indignation.

But no aggression.

I learned from her.

I replaced Gay Pride with Pride.

Cassandra and I didn't know yet that, as lesbians, there was an entire world to be adopted or aborted.

Cassandra had led a life that made me forget her age.

She got her independence early on.

At seventeen, she left Toulouse for Paris, leaving behind her parents and younger brothers.

I say "leaving behind," but Cassandra didn't leave anything.

I understood that leaving doesn't necessarily equate to rupture and abandonment.

She'd done something I hadn't dared at that age.

Leave home without blaming yourself, without it meaning that you're a shithead, without feeling, as you walk out the door during the move, and years later, as if you betrayed every one of your family values because of a single bad decision.

I envied Cassandra's selfishness, her urgent need to live life as intensely as possible, her late nights and early mornings.

All it took was weather nice enough for her to get out her summer clothes, or to recognize some ancient song in a bar, or for an old woman to remind her to enjoy her youth, and she'd keep smiling for at least twenty-four hours.

Cassandra seemed like an angel, but only in appearance.

She warned me from the start:

"Sometimes I sleep with men, but whenever I screw a guy I'm even more convinced that I only like women."

When it happened, she was usually drunk, she'd tell me about it the next day. I don't know why she told me about it.

There are things you'd rather not know.

I resented Cassandra for it.

I didn't tell her that. It was part of the game.

There were commandments to respect.

You will not tell her if she hurts you, if you feel jealous, sad, or bitter.

You will not say anything if she acts distant, if she neglects you a little.

You will not admit that you miss her when she goes halfway across the world for three weeks, that you've waited impatiently for a call but that in the end you receive two messages total.

You will not share how you feel.

Breaking these commandments would have meant accepting that we looked like something we didn't want to be.

"A normal couple."

"An exclusive relationship."

"A couple that checks all the boxes": jealousy, belonging, security, suffocation, love.

If one person fell in love, she needed to end the whole thing or be capable of hiding it as long as possible.

I didn't say anything to Cassandra.

My parents had taught me the art of dissimulation.

Of never saying anything.

Cassandra resented me for not resenting her.

I resented myself for resenting her.

I had manufactured a bit of stability with Gabrielle and Cassandra, a semblance of satisfaction and comfort.

When Nina showed up in my life, I no longer had any idea what I needed and what I was missing.

My name is Fatima Daas.
I have two Muslim sisters: Hanane and Dounia.

Between the ages of eight and ten, my sister Hanane
teaches me to perform my ablutions.

We go to our room, she acts out how to do it, without
water.

I try again, alone, with water.

I think it's fun.

Not long after, I learn how to pray.

I do two out of five prayers.

I start to pray for real, without pretending, when
I'm seventeen. Before, when I was woken at dawn, I'd
struggle to get up, tired as shit, I'd act like I was doing
my ablutions, but I didn't run water over my face or
between my toes.

I would sleep standing up as I prayed, c'mon, one,
two, one, two. Done! I'd go back to bed.

My name is Fatima.

I have a hard time letting go of one thought: I'm batshit crazy. That's why Mrs. Guérin sees me in her office.

At the start of every session Mrs. Guérin asks me if I want anything to drink.

If I'm cold, if I'm seated comfortably.

I'm careful not to cross my arms, not to fiddle with any more objects, because I know all that bullshit: body language and so on.

I face her.

I make a stupid smile, as in, I'm not going to tell you what you want to hear.

I toss back the questions she asks me.

She retorts that we're not here to talk about her, but she still answers.

I cobble something together, out of contradictory emotions.

What I say is rambling, vague, and punctuated by silences.

But Mrs. Guérin gets off when she sees that I'm tormented, when I stop myself from throwing her table against the wall, when she insists that I talk about my mother.

My name is Fatima Daas.

I turn thirty soon and I have very few memories of my childhood.

Very few memories of Saint-Germain-en-Laye.

I remember the Château Vieux, the stairs in front of the Saint Malo café. The middle school and high school students who spent their afternoons there.

Most smoked.

Almost all of them wore Eastpaks.

My sister Hanane and I used to go to Monoprix to steal makeup, to please our older sister Dounia.

Next to Monoprix, Au Nom du Pain, the bakery where Hanane and I would stop every morning before school to buy an assortment of candy from the baker with a shaved head and green apron.

When we went to McDonalds, it was a big deal.

There was a massive three-story-high play area.

We'd be all excited.

We'd talk about for it for hours when we got back to the apartment.

On Saturday afternoons, we'd go to La Charmeraie park, we'd ride bikes, we'd play hide-and-seek or freeze tag with our cousins Bilal, Younes, and Farid.

My cousin Bilal was gone a lot.
He'd come home late, he'd go out early.
He lived with his girlfriend for one year.
After the breakup, he was in jail for six months.
My aunt would claim that her son was on vacation back in the motherland.
My cousin Farid, who lives in Barcelona now with his wife and kids, used to make me repeat an expression in Arabic.
Ana ghandi kalb kbir, which means "I have a big heart."
Because of my accent, the expression would be completely transformed.
Instead of saying heart, I'd say dog.
Heart is pronounced *qalb* or *galb* depending on the region.
Dog is pronounced *kelb*.
I couldn't get the "q" out from the back of my throat.
I'd say "I have a big dog."
I don't have a big heart.

It would make my cousin laugh.
It would make everyone laugh.
Me too, in the end.

Sometimes, when I speak Algerian, people barely understand me or not at all, so they ask my mother, "What did she say? What did she mean by that?"

I don't want my mother to play the intermediary between me and my family.

I don't want her to translate me for them.

I don't want to be a stranger.

One time, they told me how Hanane had gotten lost in the park.

I hadn't been born yet.

Someone had built a cabin in the forest.
Someone used to give milk to a black cat.

The man with a limp, who sat in front of the tobacco shop every day starting at 4 p.m., was part of the town scenery.

Hanane and Dounia would make fun of him.
They nicknamed him "the hunchback."

We spent our summers at the Fête des Loges, the annual funfair.

We'd play with Barbies in the kitchen.

Younes, the youngest of my cousins, used to drive me insane.

When he felt like it, he would give me kisses on the cheek and then the mouth. He'd take my hands and put them around his neck. He'd tickle me, and also touch me all over.

He thought it was fun.

I would go hide in the living room, under the table. My mother would be busy, my father watching TV.

I'd feel like throwing up.

Sometimes I would explode. I'd shout, at my breaking point, and burst into tears.

I had a lump in my throat that didn't want to go away. But it just made Younes laugh.

The ice cream truck made the rounds starting in August.

We didn't have a sense of time yet, but we recognized it by its little ditty.

I remember that I wasn't really supposed to have ice cream, because my mother was afraid for my asthma.

It would make me cry sometimes, when I got really hot and my sisters forgot to hide somewhere to eat their cones.

One afternoon, in the neighbor's garden, I put two tiny pebbles up my nostrils to make my sisters laugh.

One of the pebbles got stuck.
At dinnertime, I ejected it by sneezing.
Which alarmed my mother.
But I just laughed.

I used to hear the social worker's name a lot: Mrs.
Brisby. We would go have dinner sometimes with a
French couple: Anne-Marie and Dominique. Anne-
Marie was a surgeon.

On Saturday mornings, we'd go to L'Arbre à Pain,
a food distribution center.

My big sister Hanane was sure that I was going to
become a journalist.
"You totally have a journalist face, Fatima."
We'd ask each other at what age we wanted to get
married.
How many kids we wanted to have.
Around twenty-five. Both of us.
A boy and a girl.

Hanane and I look a lot alike.
That's what everyone says.
When I was little I would imitate her smile.
I still imitate her smile.
People have mixed us up before, when we're out.
Hanane is seven years older than me, but she comes
across as younger.

Hanane and I always took baths together.

I have a photo of the two of us in Saint-Germain-en-Laye, in the bathtub, smiling wide.

One night, my aunt wraps my thumb in a sock so I'll stop sucking it. She tells me my teeth are going to grow sideways.

"Do you want to look like Biyouna? Is that it?"

I don't know who Biyouna is, but I don't want to look like her.

In one photo, my hair is going every which way and I'm wearing a long white T-shirt that's too big for me. My hair is short.

As a family, we watch, over and over: *Home Alone, Matilda, Edward Scissorhands, Pippi Longstocking, Mrs. Doubtfire.*

We listen to the same music: "Gravé dans la roche," "7 Days," "Sans (re)pères," "Au summum," "It Wasn't Me," "Mystère et suspense," "What's Love," "Ces soirées-là," "Les Rois du monde," "The Real Slim Shady," "Oops! . . . I Did It Again," "Trop peu de temps," "Stan," "I'm Outta Love."

I'd listen to that music on my aunt's Walkman when I was in the hospital. When my sister Hanane visited me at lunchtime, she'd cut up my meat into little pieces.

I would cry. I didn't want to eat it.

It wasn't halal. I knew it, I was sure of it.

I was in a French hospital, not a Muslim one.

My whole family made me think that it was halal.

Dounia finally told me, "When you're sick, you're forgiven. You have to eat to get healthy."

I don't like meat.

I'm not vegetarian.

My father forces me to eat lamb on Eid.

When he leaves the room, I put bits of meat in my pockets.

Later, I throw them in the toilet.

I flush, relieved.

Thank you, God.

Our neighbor on the seventh floor kills herself.

My cousin Farid uses the opportunity to steal her couch.

She was Portuguese.

Her last name was Pereira.

I stop stealing at seventeen.

It's my aunt who taught me everything.

At the *marché*, she tells me to slip hair bands around my wrist and pull down my long-sleeved shirt.

Most of the time no one notices. She congratulates me with a pat on the shoulder.

When I panic, she tells me I'm a *behloula*, an idiot.

We enter supermarkets, we drink and eat as much as we want.

I think I'm talented.

But I'm not the best.

My aunt prefers Hanane.

She hates our oldest sister, Dounia.

She makes fun of her.

Occasionally, my dad comes to her defense.

The first time that Dounia runs away, she's sixteen. We're still living at my aunt's.

That night, my father finds her in the La Défense district, with two girlfriends.

She's smoking.

He drags her by her hair.

My dad's illiterate.

He called me "my treasure" for nine years.

My name is Fatima Daas.
My affections are fickle.
Unstable.

I'm twenty-five years old when I meet Nina
Gonzalez.
She's thirty-seven.

The first time Nina opens up to me, we're in Clichy-
sous-Bois.
Across from city hall.
Nina sits next to me and sets down two coffees.
I thank her for thinking to bring me one.
I never knew if we thought about each other in the
same way, without telling each other.
There's lots of activity around us.
When I'm with Nina, I unknowingly filter out the
children gleefully sliding down the stair railing, I
pretend not to see friends walking by on their way to
Chêne Pointu, the nearby housing project, I no longer

hear the noisy conversations at l'Orangerie, the event space across the street.

Nina shares.

"My mother says that everything looks good on me, that everything I wear looks good. But really, everything looks good on me since my mother stopped dressing me."

"I wore the same clothes from age zero to eleven."

"My mother is a cold woman."

I want to react, but I use the same words every time, the same words since I was fifteen—they're not pretty, not intense, not powerful. The same stiff expressions.

And when she says "My mother is a cold woman," I don't feel like talking anymore. I feel like taking her in my arms. Instead, I look at the ground, I tear at the grass, I throw pebbles when I don't know what to do with my hands anymore.

Nina has friends who vote right-wing.

She says most of them are heteronormative thinkers but that she loves them anyway.

I tell Nina that I still have homophobic friends and that it's getting harder and harder to love them.

Nina's life story is broken up by my questions, our silences, our looks.

She tries to talk about herself and it's hard, I can tell from her body, her legs are curled up one over the other, her arms half-crossed, her head down.

I listen to her attentively, as if to memorize it all, to write it all down.

I let Nina read what I write.
She asks me one day if I regret my choice.
I answer no without even taking time to think, probably because I need to reassure her.
I regret it in the moment I send her the text.
I don't regret it the next day.
I regret it again with time.
Today, not at all.

"Have you ever been written about, Nina?"
"YES!"

Fuck! I feel like someone just stole the last spot in the parking lot.

Nina continues, "Wait, you mean have I ever written about myself?"
I reformulate my question more slowly: "Has someone else ever written about you, Nina?"
"Oh, okay. No!"
I feel the same satisfaction as when I find my phone, after thinking I'd misplaced it.

"No one writes about me. But don't you write about me, otherwise you're gonna have to say some stupid shit."

We laugh, looking at each other, sitting face-to-face, less than six inches apart.

It's like there's a security perimeter with Nina that I force myself to respect.

A virtual security perimeter that I made up entirely.

Sometimes I'm scared to be close to her, sometimes of not being close enough.

Since meeting Nina, I've written every day.

I scribble bits of sentences about all the women I compare to her, all the women I can't love.

Silence.

I look at Nina. I ask her if I can write about her, explaining that it's important to me that I have her consent.

She hedges, as she often does when I ask her something.

When she's not hedging, she doesn't answer at all. Or else she makes a joke or quotes some complicated philosophical saying that I can't figure out.

I get a telephone call, so we don't finish the conversation.

I think about it several days later but don't dare bring it up.

I think about it every time I see her name take
shape on the white page on my computer.

He had said, "You won't write a book about
me." But I haven't written a book about him,
neither have I written a book about myself. All I
have done is translate into words—words he will
probably never read; they are not intended for
him—the way in which his existence has affected
my life. An offering of a sort, bequeathed to
others.

During all this time, I felt I was living out
my passion in the manner of a novel but now
I'm not sure in which style I am writing about
it: the style of a testimony, possibly even the sort
of confidence one finds in women's magazines,
a manifesto or a statement, or maybe a critical
commentary.

I do not wish to explain my passion—that
would imply that it was a mistake or some
disorder I need to justify—I just want to
describe it. —Annie Ernaux, *Simple Passion*

My name is Fatima Daas.
I'm French of Algerian descent.
My parents and my sisters were born in Algeria.
I was born in France.

My father would always say that words are "for show," that only actions count.

He would say *smata*, which means over-the-top, to the point of disgust, whenever he saw two people on TV tell each other, "I love you."

Incidentally, I think it's terrible to say "I love you."
I think it's just as terrible not to say it.
To fail, to stop yourself.

Love was taboo in our home. So were shows of affection, and sexuality.

When my sisters managed to convince our father to let us watch *Charmed* on TV (because there was only the one television, which was in my parents' bedroom), all it took was a man's hand brushing against a woman's for my father to say *khmaj* and change the channel immediately.

    Khmaj means rotten.

My name is Fatima Daas.

I need to sustain multiple relationships.

I tend to be polyamorous.

I figured out that I'm not polyamorous.

I don't fall in love.

I don't believe in polyamory.

One morning, zoned out under the covers, I attempt to surface.

Gabrielle asks if she can tell me something.

I mumble yes, in a worried, tired voice.

"You don't sleep with me the way you're supposed to."

I don't say anything. My brow furrows involuntarily.

Gabrielle comes out of the bathroom, a white towel around her waist. She sits on the edge of the bed. She explains.

"The thing is, Fatima, you say that you don't love me, that you've never loved anyone, that you haven't fallen in love, but then, when we're together, in bed (she says this indicating the sheets), or in the shower (she says this pointing at the bathroom), the way you look at me, grab the back of my neck, bite my lips, the way you smell me, the way you put your hand between my legs, what's all that supposed to mean? You make love to me as if you loved me, but you don't. Either we fuck or we make love, Fatima. But stop pretending!"

At those words, I get up, I grab my black Kaporal T-shirt.

Gabrielle watches me, she doesn't hesitate, she takes my hand and pulls me down next to her.

She hasn't moved since the beginning of the conversation.

I look at her feet to avoid eye contact.

I think about the coffee I have yet to drink.

I feel like leaving, like calling Nina.

Like telling her, now, right away, that I've just figured something out.

But Gaby lifts my chin with two fingers.

So I come back to her.

"Don't take off, it's not a criticism. It's just that you make me believe certain things. And every time you leave, I'm afraid it's for good, that you'll decide to end everything because of your religion. And that you'll never look back."

I still see Nina's face instead of Gabrielle's.

She puts one hand over my mouth when I'm about to speak.

She knows she shouldn't bring up any doubts.

She knows it'll make me run away.

She gives me a long, passionate kiss.

I think, as we're exchanging saliva, about what she said:

"You make love to me as if you loved me."

I tell her I have to go.

I didn't drink any coffee that morning.

Gabrielle didn't hold me back.

And I certainly didn't call Nina.

My name is Fatima.

Fatima is a girl's name, a Muslim name.

I'm supposed to be a girl, so I start wearing makeup when I'm in high school.

I have long hair.

I look more and more like a woman.

The boys like it.

I don't.

I've been going out with a boy for two months.

He's Tunisian and a practicing Muslim.

His name is Adel.

I break up with him once.

He gives me some time.

We get back together.

I tell myself: "You can do this, Fatima. He's a good guy."

We go out for another month.

I try to see him as little as possible.

I cheat on him with a language assistant who works at our school. A Mexican with a unibrow and slightly slanted eyes.

I opt for honesty.
I tell Adel about it.
That's what people do, I think.
So I do the same.
At first, he's silent.
I'm afraid he'll lose confidence in himself, because of me.
I'm not afraid that he'll end the relationship.
I hope that he will.

The silence is long, hard to break.
My communication issues take up all the room.
My arms are crossed and my back tense.
Adel paces in front of me, without saying anything,
one hand on his head, moving between his forehead
and the back of his neck.

He sits down beside me.
He looks at me.
He talks to me.
I say nothing.

Adel says that he knows the best thing for me.
"You need time, Fatima!"

I feel nauseated.
We break up then get back together.
This time, I can't do it anymore.
The slightest thing he says or does annoys me.
I do my best to ensure it ends badly.

My name is Fatima Daas.

I come from a Muslim family.

I have two older sisters: Dounia and Hanane.

Hanane always used interpersonal relationships as an example of how to practice Islam.

She would say that if you love someone, you invest yourself, you give them your time, your kindness, and your attention.

You nourish the relationship.

With God it's the same, you can't love Him without proving it to Him.

I viewed my relationship with God as a relationship in its own right: investment, love, trust.

I quickly realized that I couldn't love God without knowing Him, much less make Islam my religion without a solid understanding of it.

I needed to love God and Islam to be able to practice my faith out of desire and love and not obligation.

I felt like building that connection with religion was the right approach, but at the same time I realized that I didn't really know how to invest in a so-called relationship, how to do the whole "prove your love" thing.

Before, it seemed dangerous to say truths out loud.

For a long time I thought that things were felt more than they were shown.

That's what stuck from my upbringing: show through little gestures but never say.

My name is Fatima Daas.
I studied philosophy for three years.

My mother always said that you shouldn't try to understand, shouldn't speculate or question things.

God says something, you shouldn't wait, you should do it. You should obey. For a long time, I didn't see anything wrong with that. It was my parents' religion, the right religion, my religion.

I followed that model to the letter: do what's advised and don't let doubt linger.

Overwhelmed by my thoughts, I ended up listening to Descartes rather than my mother. I decided to relearn my religion on my own, to be reborn.

During my studies, I regularly visit the mosque that's half a mile from my university.

One day, I confide in a stranger.

She's wearing a black veil that falls to her shoulders.

She's seated.

She's just finished her prayer.

A small hole in her sock reveals her big toe.

As I get closer to her, I smell musk.

It reminds me of my mother.

Two women at the other end of the room are talking quietly.

One of them is holding a Koran in her hands.

The other is stretched out on a prayer mat, stroking her baby.

I'm ready.

Salam aleykum ukhti.

"Hello, my sister."

I'm about to tell her the situation with my friend:

She does her five daily prayers, eats halal, doesn't drink.

She's careful not to lie, but she prefers women.

In the end, that's pretty much what I said.

I added that my friend wears a veil and that she's Moroccan.

I said that as if to say, It's not me!

I glance over at the two women and even at the sleeping baby, to be sure that our conversation is safe, to be sure that my Algerian voice isn't carrying too far.

The stranger says it's "not a big deal," that it happens, more often than you think, to people who don't have "a very good relationship" with their fathers. She says the door to redemption is open, that Allah is forgiving.

"Except, you mustn't turn *haram* into *halal*."

She said "you" and my legs began to shake.
I ran my wet tongue over my bottom lip, which I bit right after.

She corrected herself. It was too late, now it was awkward.

"Sorry, your friend, my apologies, really, sorry. She mustn't turn what's forbidden into what's allowed. May Allah envelop her with His divine grace and give her strength and courage, create a miracle for her—a man with feminine qualities."

I thanked her. I said I was late for class and that I had to go. I could feel that my face had turned red. I, who had convinced myself that I never blushed.

I repeated the experiment, thinking I'd find answers to my questions, in the hope that someone would make a choice for me.

My name is Fatima Daas.

My parents are Muslim but I don't remember receiving any particular religious education during my childhood.

I didn't go to any mosques, my parents didn't give us lessons at home, just a few occasional sermons once we were adults.

Those sermons, when they took place, were led by my father.

Ahmed.

My sisters and I are in the living room, sitting in a circle around a table with a flower tablecloth.

Then, my father sits across from us, he sets his coffee on the table and sinks into his favorite armchair.

He selects a subject, he says *bissmillah*.

After that, he tells each of us what's keeping us from being a better Muslim.

These moments aren't intended to increase our knowledge of Islam.

Everything my father says we already know.

I don't think anything was ever said in my family.

Silence was the least encrypted method of communication.

My parents didn't tell me who God was before talking to me about Islam.

So I got to know Allah on my own.

My name is Fatima Daas.

I'm seventeen years old.

I meet Hugo at the entrance to his building.

It's late.

I know what I'm here for.

He wants what I want, but not for the same reasons.

He has light-brown eyes and a nose that takes up a lot of room.

We lie down on his bed.

He strokes my hair.

He tells me about his day but I'm not listening.

I start to take his clothes off.

He finally makes up his mind to get on top of me.

I tell myself, "Fatima, you're gonna love it."

I try to forget myself with an older man whom I can't make myself want.

My name is Fatima Daas.
I'm the *mazoziya*.
The last one.
The one they weren't prepared for.

At twenty-three, I hear my mother tell my sister
Dounia that two children are enough.
She insists. "I wanted to stop after Hanane."

I'm sitting in the back of the car.
I don't take part in the conversation.
I act as though I didn't hear anything.
I discreetly slide my headphones into my ears
without making any sudden movements.
Too late. Dounia reacts.
She looks at me in the rearview mirror.
"We're really lucky to have you. I can't imagine
what it would be like without you."
She says this with a smile.
I make a joke to hide my discomfort.

Even with my sister stepping in, my mother doesn't take anything back.

She just says, "It's *mektoub*."

Fate.

That night I write with black ink in a red notebook: "I'm a mistake, an accident."

My name is Fatima.
As a teenager, I'm an erratic student.
As an adult, I'm incredibly maladjusted.

In eighth grade, I insult my math teacher, Mrs.
Relca.
She's twenty-three years old.
She's just gotten her teaching license.
It's her first year in Clichy-sous-Bois.

The first time I spot Mrs. Relca in the halls, I think
she's a new student.
She's wearing shorts, a white T-shirt, and a black
jacket.
I burst out laughing when I see her walk into 406.
She puts down her big black bag, takes off her
jacket, and introduces herself.

We all give each other the same conspiratorial look.
We know we're gonna *zbeul*, raise hell.

Yahya eyeballs Mrs. Relca, up and down.

I already know what he's thinking.

All the guys, who usually sit in the back, are in the front row now.

In the middle of class, Yahya makes a suggestive joke.

He gets thrown out.

We didn't see Mrs. Relca in shorts again.

My name is Fatima Daas.

I'm a teenage she-camel.

I observe the boys on the way to school.

I think I'm better.

I don't know what it means to be a boy, a man.

Or a woman for that matter.

For a long time my mother dreamt that I'd become one.

I don't like boys but I like their accessories.

I have masculine characteristics that I try to get rid of, because my mother hates them and because I keep getting reminded that I'm a girl.

Girls want to be with a generous, attentive, virile, reassuring, and protective boy.

So I try to figure out what my problem is.

After a trip, my mother leaves three jewelry boxes on my desk.

When I walk into my room, I don't notice them right away.

They're hidden between the argan oil and a Chips Ahoy! cereal bar that's been camping out on my desk for months.

On one of the boxes, there are roses drawn over a red-and-white grid.

The second box is a square with a brown bow tie attached to the side. And the last one, the prettiest of the three, is red, simple and red. It looks like a mini–treasure chest.

I open the first box.

There's a ring inside.

A gold ring with a little flower.

It's not my style at all.

I liked rings, "men's rings," in silver.

In Arabic, they're called *fedda* rings.

My father and my uncle each wore one.

Later, I'll wear *fedda* rings on every finger.

I open the second box, the third one.

Gold. Two gold bracelets.

The first with hearts, the second with flowers.

I feel like an adult who's been belatedly spoiled rotten.

I try to tell myself that I'm happy that my mother surprised me. Though there's nothing surprising about it. My mother only wants one thing, for me to know my place as a girl, for me to love what I'm supposed to love, to do what girls do, to find myself, to recognize that I am a girl.

The present is cute, that's the whole problem, was my main thought.

My name is Fatima.
The name of a sacred figure in Islam.
A name that I'm meant to honor.
A name that I soiled.

I take the 1 metro. I get off at the Neuilly–Porte Maillot station.

When I exit the metro, I cross Place de Verdun, I don't check my GPS, I know I need to turn right at a certain point to reach Rue de Chartres.

I watch all the people wandering by and think, it's really swanky here. In Clichy, we call the guys in suits "clowns," walking with their heads high, shouldering you out of the way so they can pass on the narrow sidewalks, they're squeezed into their button-ups, I'm not sure they can breathe all that well.

I hate this place, but I like the woman who works here.

I've just turned eighteen. She's thirty-two.

I stop in front of the shop. It's 5 p.m.

Ingrid's talking to a customer.

A brunette in her forties. She wants red loafers.

I imagine Ingrid in red loafers.

Ingrid's wearing a white button-up shirt and black Levi's jeans.

I notice she's missing a button around her chest.

Here, I'm sure of not running into anyone.

I hear the sound of a sink in the little side room.

It's small, stuffy, it smells like cardboard.

This space says nothing about what we are, what we form.

It doesn't make anything official.

It doesn't say anything about me.

It doesn't say anything about us.

I slink to the back of the shop.

I pretend to be looking for my size.

There's nothing I like.

The customer leaves, and Ingrid signals me to come to the storeroom. She enters after me and stands near the window. I join her.

"Did you lose a button or something?"

"Stop! Just go grab a chair."

We stick two chairs next to the radiator.

We stare out the window together. It looks onto a courtyard.

There's no one there.

Ingrid puts on music, but turns it off a few minutes later.

She doesn't look at me. My eyes scan her entire face.

There are boxes piled around us.

Ingrid's smell mixes with the smell of shoes.

I stroke her hair.

She asks me to stop. I stop.

She opens the window, lights a joint, and I step back to watch her.

She asks me to come closer.

I wait a second.

I go closer. I move the chairs separating us.

I watch her as I undo the buttons on her shirt.

"Stop looking at me like that! You're stressing me out!"

She turns around. My impatient fingers take off her shirt. I drop it on the radiator.

"I'm not allowed to look at you, Ingrid?"

I stroke her shoulders.

My tongue licks her freckles.

Her skin tastes like vinegar.

I trace her spinal column.

I squeeze her waist as I kiss her.

There's the sound of a bell. A signal is triggered whenever a customer enters the store. Ingrid goes then comes back.

She grabs her phone, to look at herself maybe.

I think about her son.

She asks me to sleep at her place tonight.

"I'll do things to you. Sex is about sharing, Fatima, stop overthinking all the time."

I tell Ingrid I have too many things in my head.

That day, I finish every sentence with "that's all."

Ingrid asks me to confide in her, to tell her about myself, to tell her what's blocking me. I can't do it.

"You're completely repressed, and you expect other people to open up to you."

She said "repressed." I'll turn that word around every which way for a week. Repressed: closed off, obstructed, oppressed, hung up, blocking something, inhibiting something...

I grab Ingrid's hand. I kiss her.

I leave the store.

In the metro, I search desperately for my headphones in the bottom of my tote bag. Everything's badly organized: sunglasses, scattered tissues, lipstick, creased novel, metro card, Ventoline.

I finally get hold of my headphones. I shove them in my ears. I turn the volume all the way up.

Lil Wayne, *Tha Carter IV.*
"Life is the bitch, and death is her sister."

On the way, I get a message from Ingrid: "I'm sorry."

I reread the message at least four times.

I end up deleting Ingrid's number. I switch my phone to airplane mode and put it in the back pocket of my jeans.

I turn off the music.
I put on the Koran.

At home, my mother can no longer stand listening to American rap all day long.

I lower the volume because I think it's disrespectful.

I listen to the Koran less and less often.

I prefer music.

My name is Fatima Daas.
The name of a symbolic figure in Islam.
A Muslim name.
So I have to be a good Muslim.

I frequent the mosque in Sevran.

I enter the prayer room. I find the imam sitting
on a chair. There's no one else there so I take the
opportunity to ask if I can speak with him.

It's Ramadan. My throat is dry; his too, I imagine.

The imam has a long red beard and small, discreet
glasses.

He's wearing a white *qamis*. It gives him an air of
purity.

He doesn't look at me.

He stares at his feet, in white socks that go up to his
ankles.

"I have a Muslim friend who's a lesbian. Everyone
thinks there's no such thing. Someone who's
Muslim and homosexual, I mean. They tell her that

homosexuality is a social phenomenon, a Western concept not adapted to Muslims. I wanted to know your opinion, what advice I should give her, what to do so she doesn't feel like she's been excommunicated."

After listening to me at length, Redbeard responds. He has a gentle voice.

"There are Muslim lesbians just like there are Christian homosexuals. God knows better than us, and we know nothing. God created sin knowing that we would sin. But homosexuality is forbidden in Islam; it must be avoided. Your friend should increase her invocations, continue her practice, and do even more: pray half the night, fast on Mondays and Thursdays. Tell her to ask God for help, to call upon Him, to repent. This will be her test."

I tell the imam thank you.

Test (n.): an event or situation that reveals the strength or quality of someone or something by putting them under strain.
To test (v.): to judge or measure someone or something.
Put to the test (exp.): Find out how strong someone is.

"Half of religion is marriage. Maybe she should marry a man and start a family."

My toes are curling in my gray socks. I scratch the back of my neck. I start to sweat, but I don't take off my jacket. I try to pull myself together so it doesn't seem like I understand my friend too well.

The imam begins to recite references he knows by heart.

God says of man and woman:
"Wives are close as garments to you, as you are to them."—Surah *Al-Baqara*

"We created pairs of all things so that you [people] might take note."

"Another of His signs is that He created spouses from among yourselves for you to live with in tranquility: He ordained love and kindness between you."

"Do you understand, miss?"

I don't dare say that female homosexuality isn't addressed in the Koran. Nor do I dare say that only the story of Sodom and Gomorrah mentions it explicitly. That there's no talk of homosexuality, but rather of men raping young men, and not of consensual homosexual relations.

I think about the Hadith—sayings that pass on traditions related to the actions and words of the prophet Mohammed—and I remain silent.

I leave with the number of a Muslim psychologist.

I spend the next few nights skimming forums, reading and listening to scholars.

I discuss homosexuality with my family.

I get carried away sometimes.

I make a slightly homophobic joke to hide.

I go home after my meeting with the imam.

I get into my pajamas.

Before I go to the bathroom, I say an invocation that my mother taught me: *Bissmillah Allahumma inni Audhu Bika mina l-khubuthi wa l-khaba'ith.*

"I enter saying Allah's name. O Allah, I seek Your protection from harm by male and female demons."

In our home, every time you use the toilet, you wash your private parts with water afterwards, with your left hand, then you dry yourself.

The toilet is in a tiny room separate from the shower and sink. I enter with my left foot and I leave with my right foot.

At the door, I say:

Al hamdu li Lahi ladhi adh haba anni l'adha wa afani.

"Praise be to Allah for allowing me to escape all that may have harmed me. And praise be to Him for protecting me."

In the bathroom, at the sink, I wash my hands with Palmolive.

I say: *Bissmillah ar-rahmani R-rahim.*

"In the name of God the all-loving and merciful."

After this invocation, I can begin my ablutions.

The purification ritual is obligatory before performing the prayer.

I wash both hands up to the wrist, three times. I check each time that water gets between my fingers, and I rinse out my mouth, three times. I use my right hand to bring water into my nostrils, three times. I wash my face, three times, then my right forearm, and the left, up to the elbow. I run my wet hands down my head to my neck and bring them back to my forehead. I rub the insides and outsides of my ears with my wet thumb and index finger. Finally, I wash my feet up to the ankles, starting with the right foot. Three times.

I dry myself as I say: *Ash hadu ana la illaha illa Allah wa ash Adu Ana Muhamad Rasulu Allah. Allahuma Jalni Mina Tawabin wa mina el mutatailiyin.*

"I bear witness that there is no God but Allah and that Mohammed is His messenger."

I go into my bedroom. I sit down.
I say *Audu Billah Mina cheitan i rajim* as I stare at the ceiling.

I prepare to do a supererogatory prayer.

Allahu Akbar, Allahu Akbar.
Ash'adu an la Ilaha illa-llah, Ash'adu an la Ilaha illa-llah.
Ash'adu ana Mohammadan Rasulu-l-Lah.
Hayya Ala-salat, hayya ala-salat, Hayya ala falah,
hayya ala-l-falah.
Allahu Akbar, Allahu Akbar.
La Ilaha illa Allah.

"God is the greatest. I bear witness that there is no god but God alone. I bear witness that Mohammed is the messenger of God. Come to prayer. Come to bliss. God is the greatest. No god but God."

I'm standing on my prayer mat. I raise my two hands to shoulder level as I say God is the greatest. I place my hands on my chest. I recite the first surah, *Al-fatiha*: Prologue.

In the name of Allah the All-Forgiving, the Most Forgiving.

Praise be to God, Lord of the universe.
The All-Forgiving, the Most Forgiving.
Master of the day of retribution.
It is You, alone, we worship and it is from
You, alone, that we ask for help.
Guide us on the straight path.
The path of those on whom you have
showered favors, not the path of those who have
strayed or incurred Your wrath.

I recite a second surah. I choose *Al-ikhlas*: Pure
Monotheism.

Qul Howa Allahu Ahad.
Allahu As-Samad.
Lam Yalid Wa lam Yulad.
Walam Yakun Lahu Kufuan Ahad.

"God: He is Allah, the One.
Allah, who alone we implore for what we desire.
He has never beget, nor was He begotten.
And none are comparable to Him."

After that, I bend over as I say *Allahu Akbar*. I keep
my head in a straight line and I place both hands on
my knees, spreading my fingers. I say *Subhaana rabi
al'athim*, "Glory to my Lord the Almighty," three times.
Looking in the direction of qibla.

I sit up, I raise my head, my chest is straight. I raise my hands to shoulder level as I say: *Sami'Allahu liman Hamida.* "Allah listens closely to he who praises Him."

I bow low to the ground. We call this *sujud*.

Allahu Akbar.
Kneeling, I place my hands on the floor in a way that, forehead, nose, and the edge of my feet (the toes) included, seven parts of my body are touching the ground.

In this position, I say: "Glory to my Lord the Exalted." *Subhana rabi al Ala.*

I shift back onto my knees and bow low a second time.

Standing, hands on my chest, facing qibla, I recite *Al-fatiha* and another surah I know by heart.

Qibla is the direction of Mecca, of the Kaaba.

I end my prayer by reciting *Tashahud shahada.* Now I'm seated on my prayer mat. I move my index finger from top to bottom, tracing a circle, while my other fingers remain curled in my right hand.

All greetings, prayers, and kind words belong to Allah. May peace and the mercy and blessings of Allah be upon the prophet. May peace be upon us too and upon all the righteous servants of Allah. I bear witness that there is no God deserving of worship except Allah, and I bear witness that Mohammed is His servant and messenger.

May salvation be upon Mohammed and the family of Mohammed as it came upon Abraham and the family of Abraham. You are of course deserving of praise and glory.

I look to my right, then to my left as I say: "Greetings and may peace and the mercy of Allah be upon you." *Assalam aleykum wa Rahmatullah wa barakatuh.*

Once the prayer is over, I beg God's forgiveness. I recite an invocation to which I add my own entreaties.

O Allah my Lord, You are Peace and from You comes peace. Blessed are You, O Allah my Lord, the All-Revered and the All-Generous. There are no other gods but Allah, He has no match, the kingdom is His, all praises are His. He is the All-Powerful. Forgive me, my Lord, my evil thoughts, my evil actions, what I might have said and done consciously and unconsciously. I take refuge with You, for You are the sole savior, alone in knowing what is in our hearts.

I love You, God Almighty.

My name is Fatima.

I think that I communicate better than before. I manage to say "It makes me happy that...," "Thank you for...," "I had a great time with you." But I still feel like I'm saying too much. Sometimes, I express my emotions with distance and reserve. Sometimes, nothing comes out. Sometimes, I get stuck. I go quiet. Sometimes, I talk too much.

One night, I'm in the kitchen with my mother.

She's waiting for Hanane, who should be home any minute.

To pass the time, she's taking the dishes out of the dishwasher.

I've just finished my lasagna.

I'm sitting at the counter.

My mother asks me if I saw my friend Yann today.

I say that he got dumped by his boyfriend, that he'd rather be alone.

She doesn't ask how he's doing.

She doesn't want to know.

Lazim i tub. He should repent.

I hesitate between continuing the discussion and completely changing the subject.

I end up challenging her anyway.

"I don't get it, Mama!"

"Careful who you spend your time with. *Hadok nass maderehomch shabak.* Don't become close friends with those people."

My mother says this in a very calm, controlled voice, like it's just a reminder, some friendly advice.

So I borrow her words.

I say that "those people" aren't hurting anyone.

As if "those people" were a foreign species.

"Those people are only hurting themselves!"

Hearing myself speak, I feel like puking again.

"God says that either you guide them on the straight path, or they drag you down with them."

My mother has already used this expression in an entirely different context.

I think that she believes homosexuality can be something you're influenced into.

I try to make my mother understand that homosexuality isn't a choice.

My mother doesn't want to understand that I'm not going to change who I see.

"God doesn't blame anyone. He's not unjust."

I think this strongly as well, that God doesn't blame anyone.

He is *Al-hakim*. Infinitely wise in all His actions. He who judges, but who is the most just and the most judicious, because He is all-knowing.

I look at my mother. I want to soften her up.

"You know there are Muslims in that category?"

"*Makènch*. They don't exist. *Machi mousslimine*. They aren't Muslims!"

I get up. I can't stand being seated anymore.

I don't want to meet my mother's gaze again.

I start to put away the glasses she's set on the counter.

I want to help her, but she's too fast.

In a few minutes, she's put almost everything away.

My mother can tell the conversation is upsetting me, so she unsuccessfully tries to salvage things.

"I feel bad for those people. They need help."

"You know what? It doesn't matter, Mama! Nowadays you can be a Muslim anything, rapist, murderer, except a man who loves another man. Right from the start, we get rid of them, we kick them out of the religion. But who are we to interfere with someone's faith and practice? And also, don't you think they'd have rather been attracted to women?"

At no point do I say the words "gay" or "lesbian"; I say "they" out of modesty. Incidentally, I realize later that my mother and I have never discussed female homosexuality, as if it didn't exist.

I finally stop fueling the debate.
I tell my mother that I'm getting sick, I can feel it, I'm cold.
"I'm going to my room, but you can come."
She's waiting for Hanane but she follows me anyway.
We talk about something completely different.
I can't help thinking about the words she said to me.

My name is Fatima.

In my house, we wait for the month of Ramadan to eat as a family.

One night, before we break our fast, my father says that he doesn't care that he never had a son. He also says that, unlike him, my mother would have liked one.

My mother says nothing.

That evening I understand I'm not who my parents were expecting.

Their dream daughter.

I'm the son they never had.

My name is Fatima Daas.
I have a weakness for fragility.
A weakness for heightened sensibilities.

Out one night with Cassandra, I run into Nina.
Nina is with a group of five.
Cassandra and I were meeting up with a friend couple.
Cass had fallen in love with this place.
She loves the red velvet, the light-brown paneling,
and the wall carvings.
We go back and forth between the garden and the
dance floor. Summer is coming to an end. Lots of people
stay outside, beer in one hand, cigarette in the other, on
the ground, sprawled on loungers, several sitting in the
same wooden chair, laughing, chatting, making out.

Cassandra and I dance together.
I can't help discreetly watching Nina.
Her movements are ardent, her eyes closed.
The way the light moves over her face is
disconcerting.

Then, immediately, I'm sick of the vibe, I don't want to be here anymore.

Nina whispers in Thierry's ear.

And without knowing why, I'm already worried.

Thierry is a friend she's known for over six years.

Nina weaves between sweaty bodies gyrating out of sync.

I feel the heat rise all the way to my head.

I button up my Hawaiian shirt as I watch Nina leave the dance floor.

I wait for her to get a ways off, then I ask Thierry what she told him.

I leave Cassandra in the crowd. I join Nina, who's sitting on a red bench that circles around the dance floor.

Nina gets into a ball, head in her arms, like the teacher would tell us to do in elementary school, when we got too rowdy.

I sit next to her.

I grab her hand.

"Are you sad?"

She nods yes.

"Do you want me to hold you, Nina?"

She doesn't answer, but she cuddles against me.

I wrap my arms around her, and put one hand on her hip. My hand moves up gently.

I can feel her fragility. It's palpable.

It's in her back, around her spinal column.

It's in her wrists, in the veins visible beneath the skin of her forearms, in her wandering gaze, in the lump in her throat, on her dry, drooping lips, in her jerky breathing.

Nina instinctively rolled back into a ball and I stayed there watching her.

"You okay?"

"Are you okay?" she shot back.

She closed her eyes. I didn't answer.

I stroked her arms, going back and forth from her hands to her elbows, from her elbows to her shoulders.

She was tense, but I could feel her letting go as I went up her spine to the back of her neck.

I looked at her for a long time before tracing her face, before stroking every single feature.

I was careful not to show any desire.

Nina whispers in my ear, "Why don't you go back to her?"

I act as though I don't understand what she means.

"Who are you talking about?"

Nina gives me a contemptuous look. She says, "Who do you think? Your girlfriend, Cassandra."

My name is Fatima Daas.
I'm the last one in the family.
The *mazoziya*.

In front of the whole class my gym teacher says:
"Fatima, sweetheart, you're not mean, you just lack
affection."

My stomach hurts.
I feel like throwing up.

My name is Fatima.

I regret that no one taught me how to love.

One Thursday afternoon, I insult my math teacher, Mrs. Relca.

I feel heat on the back of my neck.

My hands are clammy.

She doesn't say anything.

She's here, standing in front of me, like a stop sign.

She packs up her things.

One hand on her purse, ready to leave.

And I'm here too, facing her.

Powerless.

I feel like I'm making a fool of myself.

"Indifference is the worst form of contempt."

In two minutes, that saying suddenly made sense.

There were two people in the classroom with Mrs. Relca that day. Oumaima, the tallest girl in our class, and Rudy, who everyone called Rud or by the insulting French term *pakpak*.

I'm here.

Nobody looks at me.

I ask Mrs. Relca several times why she wrote me up behind my back, without even telling me.

Nobody responds.

I get closer and closer to Mrs. Relca.

I raise my voice.

Oumaima gets between us.

That made it look like I was going to smack her.

I don't know if I wanted to smack her.

I don't know if I would have, if there hadn't have been Oumaima between us.

I call Mrs. Relca a massive bitch and leave the room.

Elena, a monitor, presses her hand against my mouth, as if to stop me from doing something stupid.

Already done.

I go out to the playground.

I huddle up in a ball in a corner.

Across from me there's a window. You can see the infirmary.

Some students walk up to me.

They ask if I'm okay.

At the back of the playground, a girl and a boy are fighting.

I stand up. I punch the wall behind me.

The bell rings for the end of recess. My fist is
bloody.

Someone comes to get me.

I'm summoned to Mrs. Salvatore's office.

I go in.

Mrs. Salvatore takes off her glasses. She looks like
Mrs. Trunchbull in *Matilda*.

She tells me to sit down. I sit.

To my right is Mrs. Relca, standing, arms crossed.

Mrs. Salvatore doesn't ask me for my version of
events.

She's not surprised that I'm back in her office.

"I'm going to get rid of you once and for all!"

My name is Fatima.

I seek stability.

Because it's hard to always be on the outside looking in, looking at people, never with them, your life passing you by, everything passing you by.

Nina lets me into her place, apologizing.

I tell her I've seen worse.

In her apartment, there's a narrow six-foot-long hallway that leads to her room. In it there's an unmade bed, and under the bed, cigarette butts, and on her desk, a TV surrounded by books.

There's a guitar, and next to it clothes that she doesn't pick up.

I feel weird at her place, but at the same time I feel good.

There's something reassuring about the mess, like I've found where I belong, like it reflects my insides a little.

I'm presumptuous enough to think that I'm going to bring some order to Nina's life, when there's not any in mine, when I can't even be bothered to clean my room, to make my bed, when at my age it's still my mother who does it.

With Nina at my side, I'm not as weird. Not as crazy. Not as repressed.

It's 7:30 a.m.
We finally lie down.
Nina plays a video on her tablet. She says it'll help her fall asleep.
She puts one hand on her heart and the other on her ribs.

"Are you here because it's not working with Cassandra anymore? Are you with me because you're gonna get dumped too? How come you didn't leave with another girl? How come you didn't get some tonight? You give Cassandra a heads-up at least? Did you tell her we were going home together?"

I don't say anything to Nina.
I lie there giving her my I-don't-give-a-shit look, when I totally do. The longer I look at her, the more I think about what Marguerite Duras said in *Practicalities*:

I think love always goes with love: you can't just love by yourself—I don't believe in that. I don't believe in hopeless love affairs concerning only one person. [. . .] It's not possible to love someone who doesn't see anything attractive in you at all, who finds you completely boring. I don't believe in that either.

Nina has the covers up to her neck.
I feel her eyes going through me.

"You know, Fatima, I can't give you what you want. I get depressed and uncommunicative when I'm in a relationship. In fact, I have nothing to offer."

"You know, Nina, you speak for everybody else but never for yourself."

"And you just want me because I say no to you!"

Hearing that irritates me, probably because it contains some truth, but I can't figure out what.
In that second I understand that I'll never have Nina and that at the same time I'll continue wanting her.

My name is Fatima.
I'm a little frightened she-camel.

Mrs. Salvatore picks up a phone sitting beneath a pile of white papers.

I assume she's calling my mother.

There's no answer.

I gave a fake number.

"Your father's number?"

"Don't know it."

I answer without looking at her.

Mrs. Salvatore gets up and walks out. She leaves the door ajar.

I find myself alone in the office with Mrs. Relca.

"I'm not even mad, Fatima, just disappointed."

I don't say anything.

I can't speak.

What am I thinking when she says that to me?

Maybe about my mother, whom I'm going to disappoint again.

She has tears in her eyes.

I'm glowering.

Mrs. Relca doesn't want me to go in front of the disciplinary committee.

Mrs. Salvatore tells me that I'm lucky.

I wasn't what you would call a "bad student."

I didn't understand why they wanted to get me to leave, expel me, kick me out.

Get rid of me like an old pair of shoes.

Or maybe it was I who wanted to go.

A few days after insulting Mrs. Relca, I see my mother and Hanane show up at school.

Mrs. Salvatore closes the door behind us.

She says that I take myself for a boy, that I'm heading down the wrong path.

I'm ashamed.

I don't know of what exactly, but something in what Mrs. Salvatore says embarrasses me.

Maybe I'm ashamed of taking myself for a boy.

I'm ashamed of being reminded, in front of my mother, that I'm not one.

My name is Fatima Daas.

I know very quickly when a person is going to leave a mark on my life.

Sometimes, I wonder whether it's me who decides.

I need to control.

I need to control myself.

I need to control all my emotions.

I need to control the other person.

When Nina asks me questions about my family, I surprise myself by talking, then I stop abruptly.

I freeze.

I stare at a water stain.

An oily patch is coming through the acrylic paint on the ceiling.

My father taught me that watercolor doesn't block oily stains, that they end up showing through those paintings that everyone finds so miraculous.

"You feel like you're giving too much."

There's no intonation in Nina's sentence, so I don't respond.

I don't want to tell her that I don't talk about my family.

I can't tell her that my mother taught me at an early age to leave your problems at home, that she has a phobia of *bara*, the outside.

I can't really say who my mother is, who my father is.

I can't tell her that my parents are still together without knowing the reason, that my sisters and I have spent years trying to convince my mother to leave him, but that our wish was never granted.

That my mother never granted that wish because she thought it would destroy the family unit.

It was for us, for "our sake," that she stayed married.

I couldn't tell her either that my sister Dounia ran away for the first time at sixteen, that she was raped, that the same night my father said to her: *khchouma*, shame.

My sister was the shame of the family. She'd asked for it.

I told her that my sister was raped anyway.

Without mentioning my father's reaction or everything that happened afterward.

I didn't only feel like I was "giving too much" to Nina. I felt like I was betraying a family secret that I was a little ashamed of.

After that, I just said that I didn't want to talk about myself.

She didn't push.
Nina knew how to deal with me.

There was a long silence, but it wasn't one of those awkward pauses.
She had a tiny mischievous smile in the corner of her mouth. I could see it coming.

"So are your sisters lesbians? Have you done stuff together?"

She burst out laughing.
I laughed too.
I always found her humor too extreme, too bizarre.

Nina makes a sly smile. I think to myself that she's exquisite. And it gives me a stomachache not to be able to tell her that, for once I'm ready, ready to talk, to communicate, to do the things I couldn't all the times Ingrid asked me to talk, all the times I should have reassured Gabrielle.

When I tell Nina goodbye, I feel like it's for the last time.
In *Medicine of the Heart*, Ibn Qayyim al-Jawziyya wrote:

There's no one on Earth more miserable
than a man in love, even if he finds the taste
of passion sweet. You see him weeping in all
circumstances, for fear of separation from his
loved ones or from the desire to see them. When
they're far, he weeps because he misses them.
When they're near, he weeps for fear of being
separated. Warm tears when they meet and
warm tears when they're separated.

My name is Fatima Daas.
I'm French of Algerian descent.

I take a plane for the first time at thirteen.
My mother and my father are afraid of the altitude.
Once on board, my sisters and I are given a small
red book.
Inside, there's an invocation to recite upon
departure.

I read the translation before the phonetic
transcription to understand what I'm about to say.

Allah is the greatest, Allah is the greatest,
Allah is the greatest. O Allah, on this voyage,
we ask You to grant us piety and goodness, and
awe, and any act that pleases You. O Allah!
Ease this voyage for us and shorten its distance.
O Allah, You are our travel companion and He
who shall look after our families. O Allah, I seek
refuge with You from the fatigue of travel, from

all sources of sadness, and from all misfortune
that may strike our belongings and our families
upon our return.

At the airport, lots of relatives are waiting for us.

The two families, my mother's and my father's, are
mixed together. My mother points them out as she says
Rakétchoufihom. "Do you see them?"
I spot a crowd, arms extending to wave hello.
I hear laughter.
I notice a child seated on a bald-headed man's
shoulders.
It looks like he's missing a leg.
I smile dumbly.

As we get closer, I can't help observing the families
around us so I know how to react once I've made
it down the homestretch and find myself in front of
mine.
My models are the families that enthusiastically
greet one another. I don't realize that every reunion is
unique.

A gray barrier separates me from my Algiers family.
There's us: the tourists arriving from the country
they know well.
And then, there's "them": my family.
They are a united front.

They form a logical whole, every family thinks the same way, has the same perspectives, the same plans, the same fears, and the same desires.

In Algeria, France is both shithole and paradise.

My name is Fatima Daas.

I'm Muslim.

I have an appointment with Imam Kadir at 2 p.m. at the Grande Mosquée of Paris.

I arrive.

I'm early.

He has me sit outside his office for ten minutes.

He's still meeting with a young woman I glimpsed when I opened the door, before he asked me to wait.

She's not very tall, a little pale.

Once the door closes, I can't help imagining her hair beneath her blue veil: an icy-blond bob.

I pull it together real quick.

You're at the mosque, Fatima.

I'm standing in front of the door.

Hands in my pockets.

I wonder what they're saying inside.

I'm surprised to find myself thinking of Dounia.

When we were in Saint-Germain, she used to listen at our parents' door.

I walk down the hallway imagining, like Dounia would, multiple scenarios. The girl with the icy-blond bob wants to convert to Islam.

Maybe she has questions about inheritance in the Muslim religion or she's decided to get divorced.

It's cliché to assume she's married.

My name is Fatima Daas.
I'm the daughter of Ahmed Daas.

The sky in Algiers is clear.
It's dry, the heat suffocating.

The first few days, I explore the village where my
father grew up.
The road that leads to my grandmother's house.
A winding road, its sidewalks ruined and too
narrow.
On the way, we dodge knocked-over trash cans.
Kids running everywhere, including between our
legs.

A stone's throw from my grandmother's house,
during my stay, several merchants call out to ask if I'm
the daughter of Ahmed Daas.
Nobody had ever told me that I looked like my
father.
I didn't know anyone. They recognized me.

Algeria is a Muslim country.

Five times a day, we hear *Al-aдhan*, the call to prayer.

As I walk out of my paternal grandmother's house, I see men heading to the village mosques, wearing *qamis*: a long tunic that goes down to the ankles.

In God's house, on Fridays, there are fewer women than men.

My name is Fatima Daas. I'm a little weaned she-camel.

In Algeria, I'm the perfect granddaughter.

The one who looks at the ground, who doesn't raise her voice, who listens to her mother, who smiles all the time, who remains silent but doesn't come off as shy or uptight. I have things to say, but I'm careful not to take up too much room.

In the courtyard, I hear bleating.

I don't look for the source of the cries.

I assume they must be coming from outside.

Dounia shows me the sheep behind the big blue tarp.

I look at them one by one, but don't go near them.

Dounia can remember an Eid spent in Algeria when she was little.

She tells me that she played in this same courtyard, with a sheep she named *sabhi Vandou*.

My friend Vandou.

I think back to the sheep that my father wanted me to eat for Eid.

My name is Fatima Daas.
I was born by cesarean.
Into a Muslim family.

At the Grande Mosquée, the imam must hear the same stories multiple times a day. So I try to rehearse mine while also formulating things as simply as possible.

I got the idea doing the afternoon prayer, *Al-asr*, in the large room on the ground floor, beside the women.

Like me.

Muslims.

Like me.

The imam could open the door at any second.

It'll be my turn to talk.

The young woman in the blue veil will leave.

I won't see her again.

The imam will close the door behind us.

Heat will spread through my body.

I'll have to tell the story of my lesbian Muslim friend.

My name is Fatima Daas.

I'm the daughter of Kamar Daas.

In my mother's family, people come up, in turns, to wrap me in their arms.

Their eyes are glistening.

When my aunts kiss my mother, they cry, one by one.

When they kiss my sisters, they tell them things they remember about them.

I study my aunts.

I'd gotten to hear their voices on the phone, but I would have been incapable of recognizing them.

I call them by their first names.

Which is maybe a little *khchouma*, shameful.

I want to go unnoticed, but it's me they're looking at.

They look at the one who was born there, in France.

The one they don't know at all, whom they nickname Titi.

Who's tall and too thin.

At night, in my mother's family, everyone stays up, even the youngest.

They sit us around a big table.

Several women leave the living room, but come back with a platter.

Each time they try to make more room on the table.

I'm afraid something will fall, afraid of making a wrong move, of breaking a glass, that they'll see me as the clumsy little girl.

I'm incredibly hot but I don't dare drink anything.

Darek hna, dar manek, dar ymek, ma tkhechmech.

"This is your grandparents' home, your mother's home, your home, you don't have to be embarrassed."

I don't think that I'm embarrassed.

I'm not used to eating in front of an assembly of people.

At home, we usually eat at different times, rarely together.

My aunt Zara brings out a tagine *zitoune* that she sets in the middle of the table. We're invited to eat an Algerian dish together, without plates or silverware. It's my first time in Algeria.

My first real family meal.

At the end, we're rewarded with cakes in every color, almond roses, honeyed chestnuts, served with delicious mint tea.

Several members of my family tell me that I'm the *mazoziya*, the youngest, the last.

I like how the word *mazoziya* sounds, before I understand its meaning.

I get an affectionate welcome from my family of strangers.

My aunts are touchy-feely. My parents less so. Or not at all.

I experience my first hugs, embraces, caresses, compliments, gentle words.

I spend my afternoons discovering the city, nature, the villages, my nights talking to my cousins, who tell me anecdotes they've already heard and repeated a million times.

I like the Algerian warmth.
I miss it when I go back to France.

The imam opens the door without smiling. The woman leaves.

He welcomes me. *Marhba*.

He doesn't introduce himself, but he graciously offers me a seat, indicating a chair across from his desk.

He doesn't serve me coffee or tea.

I think to myself that surely he receives visitors at home.

Imam Kadir comes across as someone organized, someone generous.

On his desk are piles of binders and a picture frame with a photo of him and his family in Mecca.

I remember what my best friend Rokya once said: "We're only ever happy in photos."

He's stuck pink and yellow Post-its to his computer.

Out of curiosity, I attempt to decipher his handwriting, but I can't make out a thing.

It's the calligraphy of a doctor.

I can't ignore the musty smell.

I want to put a lavender-scented candle on his desk.

The water stains on the ceiling remind me of the move.

Those first days in Clichy-sous-Bois.

I dive in: "I have a friend whom I've known for a long time who has a problem. The thing is..."

I feel like I'm in the emergency room.

The illegible handwriting.

No answers to my questions, just facts, more facts.

Incomprehensible medical terms.

The imam starts his sentences in Arabic and ends them in French.

"*Keyna waḥda* solution. It's Islam, miss."

The imam is also a doctor.

He's paternalistic. He repeats that she should take the treatment seriously and mustn't stop it. Except that now, I feel as if I'm about to go into surgery to be operated on, after which they'll tell me they can't do anything more for me.

"She doesn't really like boys. It's weird, actually... it's not that she doesn't like them... it's like..."

Going into the imam's office is the same as going into the principal's office. I messed up again, made a mistake, I'm going to get in trouble.

As quickly as possible, I need to find a way to justify my actions, a way to apologize and promise that I won't do it again.

Throughout my conversation with the imam, I stare at a small white shelf just above his shoulder.

This lets me avoid eye contact.

"Boys are like friends to her...brothers...the thing is...she prefers girls..."

There are a few books on the shelf.

A Koran with a red cover.

My attention is drawn to a fairly thick book with the title *Enjoy Your Life*.

"She likes girls...But, you know...not as friends, she *really* likes them, if you get my meaning. And then, with her dad...it's tense too...so...like I was thinking... maybe there's...how can I put this?...like...a connection?"

The imam pulls on his beard every time he's about to speak.

Another compulsive tic.

Wech rahé ∂er haja bad. She wouldn't be suffering *loukèn kanète ∂arèt haja mlekha.*

"She's doing something bad. She wouldn't be suffering if it was good for her."

The imam adds, "God created Adam and Eve, not Eve and Eve. After same-sex marriage, people are going to accept marriage with animals or children."

Late at night, I repeat the imam's words in my bed.
I fast on Mondays and Thursdays.
I pray twice as often.
I listen to the Koran.
I don't see women anymore.
I don't see men either.

There are two sentences in my head that I repeat to myself over and over: Love God as if He was in front of you. Though you may not see Him, He can certainly see you.

I cry, prostrate before the immensity of God.
I tremble as I recite verses.

"My Lord, have mercy on me. I place my faith in You."

I beg God to keep me near Him.
Allah has ninety-nine names.

I beg Him using His most beautiful names.
Ar-rahman, the Most Merciful; *As-salam*, Peace,
Safety, Salvation; *Al-ghaffar*, the All-Forgiving.

God says: "He who approaches me by a handspan, I
will approach him by a cubit. If he approaches me at a
walk, I will approach him at a run."

I proclaim my love quietly, eyes filled with tears,
voice trembling, heart heavy. I swear I won't start
up again, that I'll rise to the occasion, feed my faith,
cultivate my belief and worship.

I swear but don't promise.

Still, there's that faint voice, taking up all the room.
It's as though it was a part of me, no, something
stronger, bigger, the other half of me. The half you can't
shut up.

That voice is my *nafs*—my soul—encouraging me to
be "bad."

My name is Fatima.

The name of a symbolic figure in Islam.

An Algerian name, a girl's name.

I'm twenty-two and I go back to Algeria after three years away.

My father's side of the family.

We gather in the living room to chat.

We discuss a neighbor someone glimpsed yesterday morning whose jeans were "too tight." We discuss Bilal, who got six months in prison, and his mother, who's overwhelmed.

We discuss an uncle who visits his mother without bringing anything with him.

Not even a kilo of bananas.

I'm asked how school's going, what career I want to pursue, if I'd like to stay in Algeria for good.

I just say what year I'm in at college, that suffices, nobody's looking for more than that in any case.

I don't mention the three times I switched majors, my year on unemployment...

I don't want to embarrass my parents.

"And the veil? Are you planning to wear it? And why aren't you married yet? You shouldn't wait. It's good to have children early."

Sometimes, I want to be myself. To say what I think. But my parents' words creep in.

"What will our families think when they find out that..."

"You're going to bring shame upon us."

"They're going to tell everyone..."

"They're going to ruin your reputation."

"They're all going to talk about you."

"People talk about us."

"Do you want to soil our reputation?"

I kiss my paternal grandmother on the forehead.

She has henna patterns on her hands.

She keeps a firm grip on my arm.

As soon as I stand to leave, she asks me to stay. Before, my grandmother used to tell lots of stories. She's become quiet.

She doesn't recognize me. She thanks me for coming to see her and asks me every ten minutes if we had a good trip.

"*Manné*, grandmother, that's Fatima, Ahmed's daughter. You know, your son who lives in France…"

Then, she squeezes two of my fingers. And closes her eyes.

That same year, my grandmother has a stroke.
She dies five days later.
She's eighty-eight years old.

My grandmother dies in her son's truck.
She's on her way home from physical therapy.
It's 11 a.m.
When my sister Dounia finds out, she sends me a text: *Manné died*.
I ask Dounia for Ahmed Daas's number.
I call my father.
He picks up.
He asks who I am.
In an inaudible voice, I say, "It's Fatima."
Then: "*Allah y Rahma*. May she rest in peace."
"I couldn't get there in time to see my mother alive. I hope at least to see her dead."
We hang up. I feel shivers down my spine.
My father takes the 4 p.m. flight to Algiers that same day.
I think back to the first time I wrote something.

I never got to meet my grandfathers.

They're dead, but they live on through stories. Among those that people could share with me during my visits, there's the one about the jinn.

They say that one day my grandfather was eating a piece of *qalb el louz*, a "heart of almonds," an Algerian pastry.

Sitting on a bench in the El Kettar cemetery in Bab el-Oued, my grandfather is taking the last bites when a jinn, an evil spirit, appears before him.

No one's sure in what form.

The jinn asks my grandfather to give it a piece of the cake.

My grandfather, known for his generosity, informs it that the vendor is right across from the cemetery.

As my grandfather is about to go buy it a cake, the jinn explodes in rage. He wants the last bite.

They say that the jinn put a curse on him that day.

My paternal grandfather died when my father was a teenager.

My father says that his father never laid a hand on him, even though he would hit all his brothers and sisters.

The oldest of my aunts says that he would hit all of them, but that my father must have forgotten.

My father says that his father would wake him in the middle of the night to eat meat.

My father says that his father was a man, the kind they don't make anymore.

As an adult, back in France, I write in a notebook: "It's like I'm leaving a part of myself in Algeria, but every time I tell myself that I won't be going back."

My name is Fatima.
The name of a symbolic figure in Islam.
A name that must be honored.
A name that mustn't be soiled.

I'm at my best friend Rokya's place.
Rokya, my magic.
She knows how to tell when her presence is indispensable and when she should give me some space.

Rokya and I talk about Nina for hours as we eat junk food. We mix sweet and salty, and stuff ourselves with candy.

It's like we're twelve years old again.

"How do you not get bored with all my girl dramas, Roky?"

"Stop calling me Roky or I'll knock your teeth out. You won't be so cute after that."

"But Roky is so sexy!"

"Don't start, Fat. And it's not drama-*s*, you only talk about Nina. You might be monogamous, actually."

Rokya laughs at her own joke. Her dimples come out as her grin widens.

She's sublime.

She manages to get a smile out of me.

She's always been able to, since middle school.

"You don't bore me, Fatima. Nina's special. You look at her like she's Godot. I swear, that girl doesn't know what she's losing. She doesn't know what she's missing. You want me to tell you the truth?"

I don't respond.

Rokya knows that I've switched to radio silence mode.

I listen.

"I have confidence in the kind of person you would have been with her. I have confidence in the kind of girlfriend you can be, even though you're a weirdo. Actually, you're a huge weirdo, Fatima. You have to admit it. You're awkward, you're crazy, you act like a player and sometimes you fuck up big-time. I don't know why, but with Nina I know that you would have been faithful, patient, kind. You wouldn't have strung her along. You wouldn't have run away. Actually, I do know why."

Rokya pauses for a second, a little like she's gauging the temperature, my temperature, like she wants to make sure I'm ready to hear her.

"You're in love.

You fell in love with someone with baggage.

Nina's not a bad person.

Maybe it's not the right time.

I think that she's afraid.

She's afraid things will go well.

You scare her, so she makes up reasons not to trust you.

That reassures her.

She pushes you to go have flings.

And that's brutal for you.

I know that you hate talking about what's 'deserved,' but you deserve to be loved, you deserve for someone to give you a lot in return.

And even though you act like the girl who's always sure of herself, all unattainable and detached, who doesn't get hurt, I know it's brutal for you.

Nina hasn't given you enough, but she did show you her fragility.

And that there is trust, Fatima."

I have tears in my eyes. I ask Rokya to leave her own bedroom.

She nods. She walks out. She closes the door behind her.

She comes back. She opens the door. She sticks her head in.

She says, "Open the window, smoke a cigarette, chill, and my dear, call me when I'm allowed to be your friend again."

I sit on the edge of Rokya's bed. Her white bed. Ikea.

I play Deezer on my phone. Kendrick Lamar, "LOVE":

"I'd rather you trust me than to love me...If I didn't ride blade on curb, would you still love me?"

There's condensation on the window. I stand up and write: *Sexy Roky!*

I sit back down on her bed.

I stretch my fingers as if I'm preparing to do something decisive.

I riffle through my coat pockets. I grab my phone.

I type the first letter of her first name in my list of contacts, the second letter, the third, the fourth...until I see her last name appear. Her whole name. In front of me.

New message:

Nina,

I delete. I breathe in gently, like they taught me to do at asthma school.

I breathe out.

I start over.

Nina,

Nina,

I'm sorry that this is the best I can do, but I'm not capable of saying this to you in person. Sometimes, you have to write—a message, a poem, a song, a novel—in order to grieve for a relationship.

I tried to analyze your reactions, your lack of reaction, your behavior, but everything's still unclear to me.

For all that I tried to leave, Nina, I kept coming back, because I wanted to do better. I wanted to respect your rhythm, to adapt to how you express things, to your language. I still had things to prove to you—that you're different, that with you it's different, that my shoulders are broad enough to carry your pain, that I'm a lot better with you than without.

I wish things had been simpler, Nina. Even if you don't think it's easy that I want.

I felt like I was running into brick walls and going back for more every time. I'm standing down though I don't want to. And I know that you'll watch me leave.

I'm not scared of saying this to you anymore. Too bad if it freaks you out. Too bad if you think it's too much or if it makes you anxious. You have the right to take it or leave it.

You're worthy of being loved, Nina.

My name is Fatima.

Fatima Daas.

I was an accidental pregnancy, born by cesarean.

I share a name with a symbolic figure in Islam.

A name that must be honored.

A name that mustn't be soiled.

On my twenty-ninth birthday, I go see my mother.

I open the door.

The queen is in her Kingdom.

There's a pleasant smell of musk.

A blend of vanilla and fruit.

I set my backpack on the floor.

I say *Salam aleykum*, and tack on a "dear Mama."

She looks hard at me, responds to my *salam* but
with no term of endearment.

Aleykum salam, Fatima.

My mother's wearing a green cotton djellaba with
a floral pattern, and a wool cardigan. On her feet, the

same pink slippers that my sister Dounia gave her
three years ago.

Her brown eyes are outlined in black kohl.

She's dyed her hair with henna again.

I find my mother more and more beautiful.

I kiss her, as usual, on the forehead.

It's been two weeks since I've talked to her.

She hasn't tried to call me.

She hasn't emailed.

But I can tell she's worried.

I ask her how she's doing. She responds, *Al
hamdullilah.*

She doesn't return the question. I act as if she has.

"I'm okay too, just exhausted. I couldn't sleep again
last night. And the night before either."

My mother simply responds, *Takhmem*, which
means, "to cogitate."

I give her a knowing smile.

Wech kayèn?

Whenever my mother asks *Wech kayèn*—What's
wrong?—it's a way of saying "What's new?"

And when she asks me that, I can only think of one
thing.

I want to tell her what she doesn't know yet.

But instead I say, "Oh, nothing. And you?" with
the same moronic, couldn't-care-less attitude I've
maintained since adolescence.

My mother takes madeleines out of the oven and sets them on the counter with two glasses of tea. She says she made them this morning, after the prayer, because she couldn't fall back asleep.

Like mother, like daughter.

Takhmem. Cogitate.

Then I tell myself that there's no connection between the madeleines and my birthday.

My mother responds with: "Taste one!"

There's a little ball of white chocolate inside each madeleine.

It crunches when I take a bite.

The smell of madeleines replaces the smell of fruity musk.

For the first time my mother offers to teach me to bake madeleines.

To make them for my beloved.

Gagh naṣṣ thèb lmaðlène! "Everyone likes madeleines!"

I'm just as convinced as she is that everyone likes madeleines, especially my mother's, but I don't tell her that.

Instead I innocently ask: "But if you love someone who doesn't love you back, do you still make them madeleines?"

"We don't love people because they love us back. We love them. That's it."

And when she says that, with a single, efficient sentence, I tell myself that it's time to answer her question, *Wech kayèn?* What's new? What's wrong?

There's no one else in the house. I'm alone with her, in her Kingdom.

My mother asks if I want more tea.
I'm not here anymore. I'm formulating things in my mind, thinking long and hard about every word I might say.
I don't respond.
My mother serves me another glass of tea.
She has more as well.
I ask: "Shouldn't we leave him some?"
She says not to bother.
"Him" is her husband.
My father.
Ahmed Daas.

My mother taught me to think about those who aren't there, even when you're not sure if they'll be back.
My mother tells me about a news report she saw on TV about working conditions for nurses in hospitals.

Kènt haba nwèli firmiya bessah khouya ma khalanich.
"I wanted to be a nurse, but my brother forbade it."

With lots of emotion, I tell my mother that it's not too late.

Dorka, ntouma lazem derou haja kbira bach nkoun mheniya.
"Now it's up to you girls to do great things, that way I'll be appeased."
She said *mheniya*: appeased, unburdened, relieved, consoled.
I would have preferred she'd said "proud."
But all things considered, maybe it's better to be appeased than proud.

"I have to tell you about my novel, but forget it. Not now."
I say this with the same detached tone.
Goulili dorka, waghlach tseney?
"Tell me about it now. Why wait?"
I get my impatience from my mother.
I've waited twenty-nine years. She's right.
Why wait longer?

It's the story of a girl who isn't really a girl, who isn't Algerian or French, who isn't from Clichy or Paris, a Muslim I think, but not a good Muslim, a lesbian whose homophobia is built into her. What else?

I think very hard.
It sounds wrong.
I don't say a thing.

I tell my mother that I'll let her read it later.

She doesn't insist. She opens a cupboard. I'm guessing she's going to offer me a piece of cake. I already know I'll leave five pounds heavier.

But instead, my queen takes out a notebook, with a message written in large letters, in English: PRESENT FOR YOU.

"Happy birthday, *benti*."

My daughter.

CREDITS

Fatima Daas was born in 1995 and grew up in Clichy-sous-Bois, France, where her parents settled after arriving from Algeria. In high school Daas participated in writing workshops led by Tanguy Viel. Influenced by Marguerite Duras and Virginie Despentes, she defines herself as an intersectional feminist. Her debut novel, *The Last One*, has sold more than ten thousand copies in France and has been translated into several languages.

Lara Vergnaud's translations include Yamen Manai's *The Ardent Swarm* and Ahmed Bouanani's *The Hospital*, as well as texts by Joy Sorman, Zahia Rahmani, and Scholastique Mukasonga, among others. She is the recipient of two PEN/Heim Translation Grants and a French Voices Grand Prize, and has been long-listed for the National Translation Award.